There I Find Patience

Strawberry Sands Book Eight

Jessie Gussman

Published By: Jessie Gussman

Contents

Acknowledgements

Cover art by Kim Killion of The Killion Group
Editing by Heather Hayden
Narration by Jay Dyess
Author Services by CE Author Assistant

Listen to the unabridged audio for FREE performed by Jay Dyess on the Say with Jay channel on YouTube. Get early access to all of Jay's recordings and listen to Jessie's books before they're available to the general public, plus get daily Bible readings by Jay and bonus scenes by becoming a Say with Jay channel member .

Chapter 1

She had just made a terrible mistake.

Pam Corrigan held the key that she'd been given at the closing in her hand.

What had she been thinking?

She sighed deeply and got out of her car, crossing the sidewalk and going up the steps to the duplex she shared with her best friend, Mark Shields.

Mark owned the duplex, and when Pam's marriage had blown up ten years ago, Mark had offered to allow her to move in to the other side which happened to be vacant at the time.

Pam had moved out of Strawberry Sands when she got married, and hadn't pictured herself moving back in. But with two teenage girls and nowhere else to turn, she'd taken Mark up on his offer, thinking it was only a temporary thing.

Temporary had turned into a decade.

"Good morning, Pam," Miss Heather called over. Miss Heather lived in the large house across the street with her granddaughter and her husband and several other older ladies. It wasn't exactly an assisted living facility, but it probably could have been.

Regardless, Miss Heather was a neighbor and a good one, and Pam turned, placing a smile on her face and waving across the street.

She hadn't seen Miss Heather nor Miss Daisy sitting on the porch, enjoying one of the rare warm April days.

April was just as likely to be below freezing as above eighty in Western Michigan along the lake.

So, when a person got a warm, beautiful day like today, they needed to get out and enjoy it.

Or get out and go buy an inn, apparently.

Pam swallowed again. What had she done?

"It's a beautiful day," Miss Heather spoke across the deserted street.

"It sure is. Maybe I'll be out later on my front porch, too."

"Better hurry up. I heard there's a cold front moving in, and we're going to get some rain ahead of it," Miss Daisy said, nodding sagely. "My bones agree with the weather forecast for once."

"Thanks for the heads-up. I... I need to go inside for a bit. But I definitely want to enjoy this. Who knows when it'll be nice out again." She threw up her hand and waved before she hurried up the rest of the steps and opened the door to her side of the duplex.

Some duplexes had a wall down the middle of the porch, but no such thing separated Mark's side from hers.

In the summer, occasionally his nieces had visited from Ann Arbor where Mark's sister lived. They played with Pam's girls, and they'd always use the whole porch.

Mark had been easygoing and a great neighbor, and Pam hoped she'd been the same.

They hadn't been best friends when she moved in, but through the years, no one had supported her more.

If her girls needed a daddy to go to the daddy-daughter dance, Mark stepped in.

And if his nieces needed someone to bake cookies or be a room chaperone for their senior trip, Pam had naturally volunteered.

But now...what Pam had just done could ruin everything.

She threw her purse on the kitchen table as she walked through her duplex and out the back door.

Their backyard was large and fenced in, the entire thing. Again, no fence separated between her side of the yard and his side.

They had never needed a fence.

Sitting down, she held on tight to the key that she had seemed to be unable to let go of.

Why had she quit her job again? A secure job. One with a guaranteed pension. That, along with her Social Security, would give her plenty of security even if her daughters never moved back home.

Her empty nest had been hard for the last two years since her youngest daughter graduated from college and moved out permanently.

Sure, the girls came home for holidays, most of them anyway, and sometimes for birthdays. Definitely for Pam's. But they had lives of their own, careers they cared about, and friends and hobbies that didn't include their mother anymore.

Pam really wasn't bothered by it most of the time. After all, she wouldn't want her children to be stuck at home, afraid to go out and do anything or go anywhere.

Although, she really wouldn't mind spending more time with them. And wouldn't have minded at all if they had chosen to stay at home and start their careers there.

She missed them.

Maybe that was why she had done what she did.

Was this what a midlife crisis looked like?

"Hey there."

The voice made her smile. Mark somehow always steadied her nerves. She'd been through the typical teenage drama and angst that every parent had gone through. Mark had spent more than one evening sitting at her table after the girls had gone to bed talking her down from a limb. Reminding her that everything passed, that a catastrophe today was something to laugh at tomorrow.

She appreciated his down-to-earth sensibility and the way he always made her problems seem like they weren't quite as bad as what she thought they were.

She wasn't sure how he was going to make her mother's reaction something that wasn't terrifying to her or convince her that she would eventually laugh at it, but if anyone could do it, Mark could.

"Hey," she said, trying not to sound depressed and petrified. The way she felt.

He finished walking out across his small back porch and sat down on the steps, on his side, with a good two feet between them.

They'd always been friends and nothing more. She appreciated his friendship more than she could say. Even now, knowing that she had just done something ridiculously dumb, just having him beside her made her feel... If not the smartest person in the world, at least like the repercussions of this day weren't the worst things that could happen to her.

"What's wrong?" he asked, not with alarm in his voice but with the confidence of someone who knew her.

Sometimes she loved having a friend who knew her so well that he knew something was wrong without words, and at other times, like now, it was a pain. What was she going to tell him?

"Just spit it out. I know you're sitting there wondering how you're going to tell me, and don't worry about it. Just tell me flat out."

She huffed out a breath and shook her head, looking over at him with a half-smile, half-exasperated look on her face. "Really? You have to read my mind today?"

"Pretty sure that's my job, isn't it?"

"No. Your job is to plant flowers and trees and make people's yards look beautiful. I'm pretty sure life counseling isn't in your job description."

His hands, work roughened and brown, rested on his leg while his boots were firmly planted on the step.

She always wondered why he didn't get married again. When she stopped to think about it, he was handsome. And kind, considerate, and sensitive. He was funny too and levelheaded. He had dated occasionally, different moms who were single and classmates of her daughters, but nothing ever stuck.

She wondered why.

Funny thing to wonder about now. Probably it was her brain trying to come up with a way to not answer his question.

"I do all those things, and I provide life counseling to a very elite group of people. Actually, that group includes just you."

"I can't complain about your life counseling. It's always been right on for me. But I feel bad that you even have to do it."

"I just like being involved in your life."

He was humble too. He was always able to give her good advice, because he was wise. He spent a lot of time with the Lord and in His Word, and that had a tendency to make a person wise.

"What did you do?"

"How do you know I did something?"

"Just a hunch," he said, humor in his voice.

"Well, it's a good one."

She'd done something terrible, and she was about to do something even worse.

She looked up, over the back of the fence, at the pasture that ran behind her house.

There were horses grazing in it, and the way the wind blew their manes and tails back soothed her soul almost as much as having Mark beside her.

He was quiet, knowing her well enough that he could probably read the signs that said she was trying to figure out where to start. Sometimes, it just took her a little bit to sort through the information in her brain and decide how to spit it all out.

"I quit my job."

"No." Disbelief forced the word out and wrapped his tones in shock.

"Yeah." She laughed a little, humorlessly, and lifted her gaze to meet his. "I told you it was bad."

"I knew there was a lot of stress there. But… I hadn't realized how much."

It was terrible to work somewhere where a person couldn't use their basic core beliefs to help any of the children. Things that she knew would help kids weren't allowed to be uttered in the classroom.

The previous principal at the school allowed them to talk about their faith and didn't get too concerned about it. But the new administration that had slowly been replacing the older folks as they retired had cracked down in a major way last year and this year. Being in the classroom was stressful enough, but she wasn't allowed to pray with the children, wasn't allowed to tell them that Jesus loved them, wasn't allowed to mention God at all. How did a person talk about science without mentioning God?

She always skipped over most of the parts of evolution in her science textbook. When she did mention it, she made sure to emphasize that it was a theory. In a small school like Blueberry Beach, where the school was located and where the kids from Strawberry Sands attended, folks would agree with stuff like that.

But her freedom to speak the Truth had been slowly taken away, and the stress had been getting to her. The workplace environment had gotten worse, even though there were many teachers who still got together in the mornings and had prayer for the students and Bible study together before the workday began.

Still, working in such an anti-Christian environment had taken its toll on her, along with the fact that her children were gone, and her life was...almost over. More than half over. It had been that way for a while, but the thoughts had been settling in all at once.

"I know. It's crazy, isn't it?" she said.

"I don't blame you. I don't think I could've worked as long as you did. When you're not allowed to talk about what you believe, and you're not allowed to share what you know will help the children who are having issues, it's really difficult."

She almost felt targeted and discriminated against. After all, pretty much anything else was perfectly okay to talk about.

Regardless, she tried to shove those thoughts aside.

"What did it drive you to do?" he asked again.

"I bought the inn."

"You didn't." His words were negative, but his tone held excitement. She could hear the pride in it. "I didn't think you would. But you did. That's awesome. Why are you so upset about it?"

"Because I quit my job."

"And you don't have enough money to live on and fix up the inn?"

"Yeah. What was I thinking? It's one thing to quit my job. It's another thing to buy the inn. But to do the two of them to-gether? I am crazy."

Originally, when she talked about buying the inn, her thought had been to use her teacher salary to fix it up. After all, with both kids out of school and only one of her in the house, it didn't take nearly the money to run her household as it used to. Her grocery bill was down, light bill was also. The heating was cut in half, and she probably would never need to buy another item of clothing again.

But when she thought about buying the inn, she hadn't considered that she might quit her job too. That changed things.

Chapter 2

Mark sat beside Pam, shocked.

He wasn't typically home this time of day. He had a greenhouse on the outside of town where he spent a good bit of time this time of year. Also, on a day like today where it was warm enough to be working outside, he would normally be knee-deep in a project.

But he'd been on the phone with his sister and had been concerned enough about what they'd talked about that he hadn't even thought about heading to a job once he was done. There were only another couple of hours of daylight left, and his first instinct had been to come talk to Pam. She would be home from school, and sometimes just talking to her helped him see an area that he normally couldn't.

But he hadn't been expecting her news. It made his news fall right out of his head.

"It's gonna take a lot of money to get that inn operational."

"I know."

"There had to have been something going through your head."

"There was. Just...really bad some-things."

"You're not thinking about your mother, are you?" Her mother was wealthy and liked to lord it over Pam. She'd tried to get Pam to do something other than pur-sue a teaching career. She felt like Pam could have been something a little bit more prestigious and esteemed.

Pam hadn't even wanted to go to col-lege, but her mother had insisted. There was no way that she was going to allow any daughter of hers to go through life without a college diploma.

She was that kind of woman.

So, Pam said she had chosen the career that suited her the best.

Mark knew, through the years, that Pam's mother and her money had enabled Pam and her girls to go on vacations, had enabled her daughters to both go to Europe for summer trips while they were still in high school, and had helped pay for their college education.

Her mother was generous but also controlling.

Pam had handled her with kid gloves through the years, and Mark had spent more than one night listening to Pam and offering advice.

Both of Pam's girls had moved to Detroit to be closer to her mom. And her mom's money. Pam knew it, but she hoped that eventually they'd come back.

There was a big, messy situation about an aunt's inheritance that Pam was supposed to get, but that her mother was holding hostage, and which angered Mark every time he thought of it, but Pam hadn't wanted to do anything, like go to a lawyer, because she wanted to continue to have a relationship with her mother.

"I have to admit I'm surprised."

"I know, right? This is so out of character for me." She had been holding her head in her hands, and now her arms dropped, with her elbows still on her knees.

She shifted again, hugging her legs to her stomach and rocking carefully, as though trying to comfort herself.

Mark wanted to pat her on the back or stroke her hair, the way he might do with one of his nieces.

But he and Pam didn't exactly have a touchy-feely relationship. It had been friends, and nothing more, through the last ten years. He didn't want to rock the boat. Even though, there had been times he'd wondered if maybe he could, and Pam might respond, and they could have something more than what they did.

Every time he took some other woman out on a date, for example. They never matched up to the relationship he had with Pam.

Even though he told himself to be patient, that relationships took time to nurture and grow and for people to learn the little things about him, the little things that Pam knew and did automatically. It wasn't fair to compare someone who barely knew him with Pam who'd known him for a decade.

But he still did. And they always came up lacking.

"I just couldn't stay there any longer. I told you about the little girl whose parents were divorcing and who cried in my classroom for days. How could I not tell her that Jesus loved her? How could I not give her that hope? And yeah, I got reprimanded for it. They threatened to place me on leave without pay. I guess I could wait for them to do that, or... I just took matters into my own hands. It felt like the right thing to do at the time. It felt like God was saying 'yes, do it.' But maybe that was just me. Because now it feels like a really big mistake."

"Quitting your job… I couldn't blame you. But again, buying the inn at the same time might've been a little bit much."

"I know. I have a tendency to go all in on things."

"That's true."

She did. It was part of what he really liked about her. When she was a friend, she was a friend down to her toenails. She was loyal, faithful, and there was nothing that he could ever need her to do that she wouldn't move heaven and earth to try to get done, and most of the time, she saw his need before he even saw it and was already working to do what she could to fix it for him.

Everyone should have a friend like that.

Regardless, there were downsides to having that kind of personality. Quitting her job and buying an inn at the same time was a case in point.

"Maybe you can turn around and sell the inn."

"It's been for sale for three years. I hardly think that I'm going to be able to sell it in less time."

"Good point. Although, with the way Blueberry Beach has been growing, property values are going up."

"But all anyone's going to do is raze the building. Put some kind of brand-new modern type thing in. It hurt my heart every time I thought about it, but I was busy raising my girls and didn't have time. Now I do. Not only do I not have my girls anymore, I don't have a job either."

"And you don't have the money that comes with having a job. So there's that," he said, hating to be the voice of reason but feeling like it needed to be said.

"Yeah. There is that. But I have my inheritance...if I can get Mom to finally give it to me." She didn't sound particularly happy about it.

"She told you that she would give it to you...when you got married again. She was pretty adamant about the fact that you weren't getting it any time before that happy occasion occurred."

"Marriage isn't a happy occasion. Marriage is a ball and chain. I hate marriage. Marriage is the worst thing that ever happened to me."

He shouldn't have gotten her started. Even though her divorce happened ten years prior, she'd been adamant about the fact that she was never getting married again. Her husband had been a narcissist who was the charming kind, who could con pretty much anyone into anything, and had kept Pam on a string for years.

She'd probably still be on that string if he hadn't cheated on her. But he had and had left her to make a new family with someone else.

Sometimes he wondered if maybe Pam wished she wouldn't have found out about her ex's affair. Life had been a lot harder for her after her divorce.

Mark had done what he could to try to be a dad to the girls, since their own father didn't want to have anything to do with them. He'd gone through three or four more women in the years since, from what Mark understood. Pam didn't keep up with them, but every once in a while, she'd mention it.

"I don't blame you. I guess I wouldn't get married again either." Not unless the right woman came along. He'd be a lot more picky this time around than he was the first time. She was going to be...someone like Pam. Not someone like his first wife, who was beautiful, delicate, and sweet, until she didn't get what she wanted, and then she was very much like a two-year-old pitching a fit in the grocery store because her mom wouldn't buy her candy.

It amazed him that someone who looked so sweet and innocent could become so nasty and ugly over stupid stuff. Stuff he didn't understand. Eventually, he thought maybe it was him, since she'd been happily married since her divorce from him and had two children with that guy.

Good for them.

Mark just figured he was bad at picking women and had put his heart and soul into making his landscaping business a success.

And doting on his nieces. Who were now grown up and had moved away. He still kept a close relationship with them and his sister though.

"It's been long enough that Mom might have forgotten, or maybe she changed her mind. I can't believe I'm even considering this. But conditions had gotten so bad at school that... I felt like I didn't have a choice. And I truly did feel like this was something the Lord wanted me to do. I... I wouldn't have done it without that feeling. Of course, sometimes I want to do something so bad that what feels like God's leading is probably just me wanting it that bad."

"Yeah. I get that." He supposed that a person could get desperate enough to do pretty much anything.

For him, he'd have to be really desperate before he went to Pam's mom and asked for anything, but despite how much trouble she'd given Pam through the years, he knew Pam still loved her. Still wanted to have a relationship with her. Still wanted her mom to finally someday say that Pam had done a good job.

She was still waiting for that to happen. Mark wasn't sure it ever would, but he wasn't going to fault Pam for her optimism.

"You know, it's odd that you'd be here on such a beautiful spring day." She turned to look at him, her eyes narrowed. "What's going on?"

He grinned a little, her question echoing his from earlier. Probably born out of the same thing. They'd been friends long enough that they knew each other so well that they could pretty much read each other's minds. That kind of thing didn't happen overnight. It only happened when a person spent a lot of time with someone, knew them well enough, and cared to get to know them. He spent a lot of time with people over the years who couldn't say the first thing about him, because they just didn't care to learn. Of course, he'd been guilty of knowing people like that too.

That was something Pam was really good at. She cared about people, and she didn't just say she did. She showed it.

She definitely helped him in that area. He'd been rather blind about people and his effect on them when he and Pam had first started hanging out.

He liked to think that maybe there were some things that he had helped her with.

"Are you gonna tell me?" she asked, giving him a look that said that she knew that his mind had gone in a completely different direction.

"You got my mind off my problems. Now you want me to focus on them again?" he asked, only partially teasing. It was nice that he'd been able to come and talk to Pam, and somehow, she always made his problems seem like they weren't as big as what he felt like they were. Even if it was because her problems seemed bigger.

"Just because my problems overshadow yours doesn't mean that yours isn't as important."

"No, but it means that I wasn't thinking about mine. Which I appreciated, but now that you forced me to confront it again—"

"That's ridiculous. I didn't force you to confront anything. You're going to have to think about it at some point, and it'll be easier if you talk to me about it first."

"You're right about that," he said, becoming serious immediately. He could do that with Pam. He didn't have to be funny or joking all the time. It was okay for him to be himself around her. "My sister asked for a favor today."

"Oh. What are you doing for her?" she asked right away, knowing that he never turned his sister down. He always did his best to try to help her out however he could. They'd been close growing up, and he spent a lot of time with his nieces, both during her divorce and after it, helping her out however he could. Their parents had moved to Utah, for his dad's job, and his sister and he had stayed in Michigan, even though his sister was down in Detroit.

"I'm not sure I'm going to do it," he finally admitted.

"You're not?" she asked, with all the shock in her voice that he would've expected. He couldn't remember the last time he'd told his sister no.

"No. I'm not. She... Do you remember Stacy?" he asked, cringing a little at even mentioning her name. She did not invoke good memories.

"Your sister's best friend? The one that was here... Was it three summers ago? Four? She took Bruno to the pound and somehow managed to kill all of the plants in the greenhouse. That Stacy?"

"That's the one." It wasn't a happy summer. And it was only two summers ago.

Bruno was the dog that had been with him for almost fifteen years. He was old, and decrepit, and a little senile. He peed on Stacy's bag or something, and Stacy had gotten mad and loaded him up and took him to the pound.

That had been the final straw that it took for him to tell his sister that Stacy was moving out.

They were both schoolteachers and had the summers off. They wanted to stay at his place, near the beach, for some relaxation. He didn't mind. He often hosted his nieces, and he had three bedrooms upstairs. He only used one, and he didn't care who stayed in the other two. Unless they took his dog to the pound. Or killed all his plants. That had been hard to recover from, from both a personal and business perspective.

"I can't believe that she would even suggest such a thing. I mean...wow."

"Apparently Stacy needs a place to spend the summer because they're redoing her apartment. Paulette wanted me to open up one of my rooms for her. Honestly, I'd share my house with anyone. But... And I don't believe in holding grudges, I mean, you've got to forgive and forget. But..."

"That woman doesn't know what boundaries are. You don't take someone's elderly dog to the pound. And I'm not even sure what she was doing in your greenhouse."

"She said she was watering the plants. She just watered them with my herbicide. I mean, that was an honest mistake, but it was an expensive one too."

"She never offered to pay?"

"She did not."

He tried to keep the bitterness out of his voice. He didn't know Stacy's financial situation. But she seemed to live fairly well on whatever money she made, always wearing nice clothes and eating well while she was there. Plus, he'd seen her apartment. It was extremely nice, in a gated community, with all the amenities.

"Well, is there a way you can let your sister down easy? I mean, I know she loves her best friend and everything but... I guess you don't have a dog anymore."

"No."

Bruno had come back, just as feeble as ever, and had passed away two days later. He hadn't had the heart to get another dog. He just wasn't ready.

Or maybe he was too busy. He definitely didn't have time for a puppy. That was a lot of work, and he was gone sometimes fourteen or sixteen or more hours during the day in the summer. In the winter, he could probably swing it, but he just wasn't sure if he wanted to do that again. He...was getting older.

"So are you going to say yes to her?"

"No. I know Stacy is her best friend, but I just can't let her come back. I haven't figured out how I'm going to tell Paulette though. She was pretty adamant, and she's right. I am not using the two extra rooms upstairs."

"Your nieces aren't coming back at all this summer?"

"Paulette says they're not. She ought to know, since she's their mom. Apparently they reconciled with their father."

"That's nice. She spent all the time and money to raise them, then they grow up, and all they want is their dad."

Her voice held a little bit of bitterness. That had happened to Pam. Her husband hadn't wanted to have anything to do with her kids while they were growing up, but after they were out of the house and were successful on their own, he'd walked back into their lives. Pam thought it was because they could offer him prestige. He could show them off and tell everyone what wonderful children he had, when he hadn't had anything to do with the way they turned out, other than dumping them on her.

He couldn't blame Pam for being bitter, but he knew she was working through it. Trying to not hold that against him.

It was amazing that some people were able to get along with their exes. Have good relationships, even be friends.

That would never happen with him. And he doubted it would happen with Pam

either. Maybe that made them bad people.

He wasn't solving any problems, but at
least sitting with Pam made him feel better. She had an insurmountable problem, and so did he. If nothing else, they
could commiserate and support each
other. Even if they didn't figure out any
solutions.

Chapter 3

"This food is delicious," Pam said as she sat at the diner, talking to her friend, Eleanor.

They had a standing lunch date once a month, on the first Saturday of the month.

"It's Griff's special this week. I've had it once already, and I couldn't wait to come back and have it again. I hope they add it to the menu permanently." Eleanor held a forkful in midair before she closed her eyes and put it in her mouth.

"Griff sure knows how to cook."

Pam almost canceled their standing date. She wasn't sure how she was going to pay for everything, and she really didn't have money to go out to eat, but she figured she'd talk to her friend about it today. Although so far, they'd talked about Eleanor's wedding, and how married life had been, and how much Eleanor enjoyed being married.

Pam was over twenty years older than Eleanor, but they had a love of horses in common, and a love of animals in general.

Although Pam was currently animal-less, since her daughters had moved out and taken the pets that they had with them.

Pam thought about getting another one, but...she just hadn't yet, she supposed.

Maybe she could take in the Great Pyrenees that hung out around town. She hadn't seen him for a while.

"Do you know what happened to the white dog that used to walk around town?"

"I don't know. I saw him just before Franklin's charity gala, and I think I saw him a couple of times over winter, but whoever feeds him maybe took him in for the winter. It was a pretty bad one."

They had a record amount of snow in February, but the warmth of March had made everything melt. It was still muddy, and the rain that they just had the past couple of days hadn't helped anything.

It had suited Pam's mood though.

"We don't have to do this on Saturdays anymore," Pam said, looking at her food studiously. She didn't know how else to break her news.

"We don't? Is there...something you're not telling me?" Eleanor asked right away.

"I know Saturdays are often your busiest days, since you have your clients who work during the week bringing their pets in, so it would probably work for you better if we did it on a different day."

"But Saturday was the only day that works for you because you teach school the rest of the week." Eleanor paused. "Unless you don't teach school any-more?"

"I quit. Two days ago."

"Without a notice or anything?"

"Yeah. They were going to suspend me without pay because I talked to a girl in my classroom who was crying. I told her about Jesus. I got in some big trouble for that, there was a huge backlash, and I just resigned."

"I've heard about some of it, but I guess I've been kind of preoccupied with set-tling into married life. I'm sorry. I didn't know."

"I don't think it's been in the papers too much. Blueberry Beach isn't a huge school. Most of the parents are small-town folks with those values, and they would be upset about it. I think this type of thing goes on a lot more than what we're aware of. It has to. How can Christians teach in the school and not talk about God?" She knew there were still Christians in the school. And she knew there were Christians who followed the rules. But as a Christian, God commanded that they talk about Him. How could they follow God's commands and still work in an area that didn't allow them to do that?

She supposed it was a moral dilemma, or maybe something that each individual teacher would have to have an answer for. But it was kind of shocking that in their country, this was what it came to.

She would never have thought that about the United States. Not when she was growing up anyway. Things had changed, a lot. Sometimes she couldn't believe how much.

She also knew, before she got herself all depressed, that God was in control. And He knew exactly what was going on. Sometimes, when a people was persecuted, they had a tendency to cling more tightly to their faith, to deepen it and to grow it. God knew that too. Maybe that's what His intent was. Maybe too many people in America had become surface Christians, not really caring about their faith, or about God, or about sharing it.

Maybe they needed a little persecution to cause them to dig in deeper and grow.

Whether that was God's intent or not, that seemed to be happening to her. After all, she had definitely stepped out in faith.

"What are you going to do? You don't get unemployment when you resign, do you?"

"No. I... I bought the inn."

"You didn't!" Eleanor smiled. "You've been talking about that for years. I am thrilled for you. Except... It's going to take a lot of money to fix it up."

"I know. I'm going to talk to my mom."

"I'll pray for you." Eleanor didn't have to say any more. Eleanor had met her mom, and typically after her friends met her mom, they tended to avoid her when her mom was around.

Her mom was not the easiest person in the world to get along with.

They talked for a while, with Eleanor sharing all of Pam's excitement about the potential for the inn. It was a huge job, though, a huge undertaking, and not one that Pam was going to be able to do by herself.

She had talked to Mark about it, since he was pretty handy, and in the winter, he wasn't very busy. If she spent most of the summer working on it, she knew he'd give her a hand this winter once his landscaping business slowed down.

They might be able to have it open next year this time.

But she had no idea what she was going to do to support herself until then if her mom didn't get on board with giving her the inheritance she was supposed to get from her aunt. Finally.

She didn't burden Eleanor with all of her financial issues, but they just dreamed together about what a beautiful place the inn could be, if she was able to do everything she wanted to.

When did that ever happen?

She was going to try to make it happen, she thought to herself as she bid Eleanor goodbye, the food in her stomach feel-ing warm and happy. Despite the tight ball in her chest when she thought about calling her mom.

She might as well do it now. Deciding that she would walk along the beach and talk to her mom with the sound of Lake Michigan soothing her as she did so, she headed in that direction, pulling her phone out of her pocket and dialing her mom's number.

"Hello, darling." Her mother's cultured voice came on the line.

"Mom. Hey. How are you?"

"I'm fine. Both of your daughters are here. Why don't you come as well? Then we can all be together."

She didn't know her girls were visiting their grandma. Even though she'd just talked to both of them the day before yesterday. She hadn't mentioned that she'd quit her job though. There were just some things that were hard to say.

"Tell them I said hi. I'll call them tonight."

She tried to call them every other day or at least three times a week. She didn't want to overwhelm them, and usually her calls didn't last super long. Her girls loved her, they just...needed to spread their wings. At least that's what she told herself. She couldn't imagine leaving Strawberry Sands, although she'd done it once herself.

But she'd thought she was in love. She left the town that she loved because she loved a man, and she thought he loved her.

Turned out she was wrong, on both counts, leaving and loving.

So she'd come back.

There was a lot of pain involved in all of that, and she cringed as she thought about her girls going through the same thing.

That was life. Pain and experience being great teachers, and eventually wisdom came out of all that. She wouldn't want her girls to not be wise, and sometimes there were hard lessons to learn first.

She did a little bit of small talk with her mom, discussing her mom's latest charity and the things that she and the girls were going to do that day.

Apparently they were spending the weekend. Which was nice. At least Pam told herself that. It had been months since either one of them had come to spend a weekend with her. She tried not to let it bother her and just be happy that they were spending time with their gram.

"Well, I suppose I'll get back with the girls. We have a lot of things planned for today," her mom said. She didn't really expect her mom to be able to read her mood and know that she called for something more than just catching up.

She took a breath and plunged in. "I actually wanted to know about my inheritance."

"My sister left me in charge of it. I know it's yours, and I'm not spending it. But I have to tell you that the same thing applies from the last time we talked. You get married, you get it. You don't get a cent before."

"But you know it's mine; you just said it was. I don't want to get married again."

Her mom had been in charge of dispersing the inheritance, since her sister had given her that role. Her mom was straight as an arrow and very honest. There was no doubt in Pam's mind that she would eventually get the money. It was just that her mom didn't see any problem with putting stipulations on it first.

"You cannot possibly be happy up there in that duplex by yourself," her mom said, saying "duplex" like it was a dirty word. "I'm only doing this for your happiness. And because I love you. You know that, sweetie."

"I understand that you think that's going to make me happy, but you don't understand that I don't want to get married again. I have—" She stopped in the middle of the sentence, suddenly, for some odd reason, thinking that if she convinced her mom that she didn't want to get married, and her mom wouldn't change her mind about giving her her inheritance before she was married, it was going to be very difficult to convince her mom that she was married, if the opportunity presented itself, oh, like to-morrow.

Which was ridiculous. Of course she wasn't getting married tomorrow. There was no way. Except... She'd heard of someone else getting married... It was called a...marriage of convenience. The person that she heard about had actually fallen in love.

But who could she have a marriage of convenience with...

Mark. Mark would do it with her. He knew how much her inheritance and fixing up the inn meant to her.

"Pam, are you okay?"

"Yes. I just... I just realized that I probably should never say never, because there is this guy."

Her mom knew all about Mark, so Pam didn't want to say anything else. If she mentioned that she and Mark were an item, her mom might ask her about it the next time she was in town, and Mark was the only one of her friends who didn't avoid her like she had the pox when her mom was around.

"There is?" Her mom's voice couldn't have been more shocked. "Who? When do I get to meet him? How serious are you? Are you together?"

"No," she said and then rolled her eyes. She'd never done anything like this in her life before, never insinuated that there was someone when there really wasn't anyone. Never considered what she had just thought about with Mark.

She recoiled from the thought, even as she thought that it might be...okay. And technically speaking, she was kind of living with him. In the same house, even if it was a duplex.

Still, she couldn't even go there with her mom. Or with anyone. She didn't want to lie.

"No. Nothing like that."

"I want to meet him at any rate. How soon can I? The girls and I might cancel our plans for today, and we could come up."

"No, Mom. It's nothing like that."

So all of the things that her mom had been telling her didn't have to happen. In other words, they could have come and visited with her. Even as she thought that, she realized she could go over. She didn't have to stay here. There was nothing keeping her. Not since she quit her job. Nothing keeping her other than a lot of work, an inn that needed to be repaired so she could start making money with it.

"All right. Well, if you change your mind. Let me know."

"Mom. About my inheritance."

"When you're married, we'll talk." Her mom's voice was firm, and she said the words slowly and clearly. "I love you, sweetie. Gotta run." Her mom hung up the phone.

Pam checked her screen, just to be sure, before she dropped her hand beside her and breathed out a sigh of frustration as she looked over the water.

That call did not go the way she hoped it would.

The complicated relationship between her and her mom, and now her and her daughters and her mom, made her want to give up.

Her mom had helped her when her kids were growing up. She'd provided financial assistance any time Pam needed anything, which hadn't been often. She'd paid for several vacations, but Pam hadn't asked for that. It had been something her mom had wanted to do, and the four of them had had a good time.

Her mom could be fun, but it was so easy to make her angry that being with her could sometimes be...like walking on a landmine.

Usually looking out at the lake, watching the waves roll in, soothed her soul and reminded her that God was in control.

She supposed it still did today, but she couldn't help but wonder what in the world God was thinking. Or maybe, she should be wondering how in the world she'd managed to mess things up so badly. She thought she was doing ex-actly what God wanted her to do. How could she work at a place where she couldn't even mention the word Jesus? Unless she was using it as a swear word?

There was no way she could stay in a place like that. Right? God surely didn't want her to stay there. How could she be a missionary when she couldn't talk about Jesus?

But now that she quit, she wasn't sure whether maybe she hadn't been too hasty and done the wrong thing.

Buying the inn... It seemed like a really good thing to do. Another thing that she'd been thinking about for years, and God seemed to nudge her about, but yet... Look where she was. Jobless, with an inn that was going to need a lot of money, or else it was going to be a waste of the money that she already spent.

It had taken every cent of her savings to purchase the inn. At least she didn't have a payment.

With that thought, she decided that maybe walking up the beach and going to see the inn might make her feel a little better. Although, it was just as likely to make her feel overwhelmed. Regardless, she turned to her left and started down the beach.

Chapter 4

"It's always fun to take a ride, thanks," Mark said as he got off the horse and spoke to his friend, Luke Landry, who owned the mounts they'd been on.

"It's good to get them back in shape. Most of these guys have been idle over the winter, and sometimes they're a little spooky when you bring them out in the spring. You helped me out. I appreciate it."

"Not a problem," Mark said. "It's always a bit more fun when they give you a little sass."

"Not everybody thinks that way," Luke said with a grin.

Mark raised his hand in farewell and walked out of the stable. A Saturday afternoon ride was just what he needed. He'd finished one job this morning, and rather than try to get started on something else with the few hours of daylight he had left, he'd answered Luke's call and jumped at the chance to take a ride along the beach. There was something soothing about the waves and the horses and the promise of spring. It was in the air everywhere; he loved this time of year.

His phone buzzed his pocket as he hit the sidewalk, and he pulled it out, seeing it was his sister.

"Hey, Paulette. What's up?" he said, nodding at Sunday and her husband, Noah, as they walked into the diner.

Great smells wafted out, and he thought about stopping.

Instead of that, he turned around and walked back toward the beach. Maybe he'd grab a bite at the diner after he got off his call.

As he turned, he saw Pam walking down the beach in the distance, and he thought that maybe she was heading toward the inn. It was faster if she walked around the pasture on the other side, but if she wanted to walk next to the lake, that was the way to go.

Maybe he could take her supper.

"Mark, you do know that you're my favorite brother, right?"

"Stacy is not staying the summer." He wanted to be firm about that.

"Mark. Please. She doesn't have anywhere else to go. She... I know she's a little spoiled—"

"A little spoiled?"

"Listen, I'm sorry about what she did to Bruno."

"I know you're sorry. The problem is, she's not."

"He ruined her expensive purse. I forget what kind of purse it is, but it's like thousands of dollars. Seriously."

"All right. That was a bad thing, but she left it sitting on the kitchen floor, right beside where he lays down. And he was trying to get out, but he's old and couldn't make it."

"Can you guys just admit the both of you are wrong?"

Mark bit the insides of both cheeks. He didn't think he was wrong. It was his house, his dog, and Stacy was a guest. Yes, his dog shouldn't pee on her purse, but her purse wasn't sitting somewhere it belonged, and just because Bruno did that did not mean that she could steal his dog and give him to the pound.

But arguing with his sister wasn't going to fix any of that.

"I don't know if I can get to that point, but I guess I don't want to argue about it anymore. I just don't want Stacy at my house."

"Mark. Usually you're the first person to volunteer to help. I already told her you'd be happy to have her living there this summer."

They'd already been through this. Multiple times. And it was funny how Paulette could appeal to his soft side, because he wanted to be kind. He wanted to be someone that opened their house to anyone. But not Stacy. Anyone but her.

"Look, I have to go. But maybe I can keep an eye out for another house for Stacy to live in."

"Mark. She needs you."

"Let me think about it."

"You don't have much time. School's out here at the end of May. That's four weeks."

"All right. I'll keep an eye out for some other place."

"Get a room ready for her. Please? After all, you want to be a good example to your nieces."

He did. That was the one big regret about the marriage that didn't work out. There had been no children, and he'd always loved having his nieces. He hoped that someday he'd get married again and have kids of his own, but that ship had sailed. A man in his early fifties was too old to start having children.

He was probably too old to think about any kind of romance either. But...he'd always held out hope that there was still someone out there for him.

Lord? I'm waiting.

He thought he'd been waiting patiently. But he would've thought that God would have brought someone around by now.

He supposed since He hadn't, he might as well face the fact that He probably wasn't going to.

Sighing, he turned and went back to the diner. Last week's special had been so popular that Griff was making the same food again today.

Mark would get two meals, take them to the inn, and talk to Pam, who, as far as he knew, still did not have a solution to her problem either. They could commiserate together.

Chapter 5

Pam walked around the inn, a notebook in her hand, the list she'd made already longer than two pages as she continued to think of the things that she needed to do.

This was too big of a job for her. She had no idea what she was thinking when she thought that she could just buy an inn and fix it up and start making money with it.

It was the dumbest thing she'd done in a long time. Since she'd gotten married and thought her husband would love her forever.

Plus, she missed the kids at school. Missed seeing them every day. Missed the knowledge that she was touching the future by encouraging young minds, teaching them things they would use for the rest of their lives, watching as understanding dawned and the smiles spread across their faces as they mastered a difficult concept or managed to pass a test they thought they were going to fail.

She resented the fact that she'd been basically forced into resigning, rather than getting fired.

She also resented the fact that she couldn't talk about the most wonderful thing that had ever happened to her, and yet there were so many nasty things that teachers were required to actually teach, not just talk about. It seemed like the world was backward and upside down, and there was no common sense left.

She tried to shove those thoughts aside. Being bitter and angry wouldn't help anything.

Although neither would being overwhelmed and discouraged.

She let the hand holding the notebook drop to her side as she stood at one of the windows in the big open gathering area on the third floor and looked out at

Lake Michigan. It was deep blue today, reflecting the springtime sky, and mostly calm. It was beautiful, stretching out into a hazy mist at the far horizon.

She could sit here and look at that view forever.

If only she could afford to. She had to do something to earn money. She could hardly get her old job back. Although the idea of never teaching again made her very, very sad. She had been born to be a teacher.

Interestingly, Mark had gone to school to be a teacher, and he thought that he'd be a teacher during the year and run his landscaping business during the summer. It turned out that landscaping was a lot more profitable than teaching, and it took more than just the summer. He'd start as soon as the snow started melting in the spring doing yard cleanups and planting spring bushes. And his work continued until late in the fall, when he again did yard cleanup, raking leaves and doing fall plantings.

She often teased him that when he got older, he'd have to go back to teaching, and in the last few years, he'd laughed along with her and told her that he thought about it.

She supposed she should worry a little more about him, since the work that he had was backbreaking and hard and he wasn't getting any younger.

Neither was she.

She smiled as she thought about him. Maybe, she'd just give up on the list and see if she could go find him and they'd get pizza for supper or whatever the diner had on special.

Almost as though her thoughts conjured him up, she glanced down and saw a man carrying a bag and walking up the hill toward the inn.

It had to be Mark. She recognized that confident stride and the easy swing of his arms.

Smiling, her discouragement lifting just at the thought that he was coming to see her, knew she would be here, and had brought something—she hoped it was food. If he knew her as well as she thought he did, it would be food.

She hurried down the steps, since although there was an elevator, it wasn't working.

So many things weren't working. She had been crazy to think that this was a good idea.

She made it to the door just as he did and opened it as he raised his hand to knock.

"Why didn't you talk me out of this?"

"I thought that might be what you'd be thinking. I brought food."

"Have I ever mentioned how much I love you?" She breathed deeply. "It smells like sausage."

"It's something that Griff is calling smoky kicky Italian sausage pasta. It's supposed to be pretty good." He grinned a little at her. "It's interesting to me to see that you're assuming that I brought some for you."

She paused in the act of opening the door. "You better have. Or I'm eating yours."

"And here I thought you were going to throw me out. If that's all that's going to happen…"

She laughed as she opened the door and he walked in. It was a little chilly out with the breeze, but the temperature inside the building, despite the fact that the heat was not on, was perfect.

"You want to go up to the third floor? There's a big great room up there. I guess it was a common area or something, and the view is awesome with the floor-to-ceiling windows."

"Sure."

"You're going to have to climb the steps, since the elevator isn't working."

"I dunno. I'm getting kind of old."

"All the more reason to get more exercise. It keeps you young."

They laughed as she led the way to the steps and they climbed the stairs together.

"It's pretty dark in here," he said as she led the way with her flashlight.

"There's a stairwell on the other side, and it has skylights, which keeps the entire thing lit even though the lights aren't on. I think this one actually has skylights too, but maybe they broke or something, and they put plywood over them. At least, that's what it looks like from what I can tell. I haven't actually gotten a ladder and gotten up on the roof."

"And you're not going to do that either. Correct?"

She ignored him. If she had to get a ladder to get out on the roof, she would.

"Pamela Corrigan. I expect an answer."

"You didn't use my middle name, so I don't think you're serious."

"Pamela I'm-as-stubborn-as-this-stick Corrigan, tell me you're not getting a ladder and going out on the third floor on the roof that is three stories above the ground. Especially by yourself, with no safety equipment."

"I won't do it with no safety equipment. How's that?"

"Your idea of safety equipment is probably... I don't even know. But I hardly doubt that it's OSHA approved."

"Yeah. Definitely OSHA would not approve of my methods."

"Exactly. So, I need a promise. Right now."

She smiled at his demand as they reached the top of the stairs and she pushed open the door. "I'll let you know when I'm doing it, that way I won't be alone."

He didn't say anything for a bit as she led him down the hall to the area where it opened up to the floor-to-ceiling windows that faced the lake.

"Whoever was building this really knew how to take advantage of a view," he murmured.

"Right? This is just absolutely amazing. It's such a shame for it to be going to waste like this."

"Crumbling into ruins," he agreed with her.

He brought plastic silverware, and they settled down, sitting on the floor side by side staring out at the lake with their food in front of them.

Mark prayed for it, without them really talking about it. They'd eaten plenty of times before, and he always said the blessing.

It was so nice to be with someone that she felt so comfortable with. Although, it hadn't been like that to begin with. It had taken years for them to fall into a routine.

She supposed there were some people who met each other and felt like they'd known each other for years, but the friendship that she and Mark had had been built on years of chance encounters, being neighbors, and eventually becoming friends, then good friends, and now she would consider him her best friend.

It hadn't been an overnight thing.

But that was how some friendships grew. Over time, as they shared experiences and went through life together.

"Have you heard from your sister again?" she asked as she opened up her Styrofoam container and paused with her fork above the saucy-looking pasta. It smelled amazing. She sat, just breathing in the scent while Mark let out a sigh.

"She's offended that I won't let her best friend come and stay with me."

"But she's still talking to you?"

"Yeah, she called just before I went to the diner to get comfort food and figured you'd join me in eating my troubles away."

"You know I am always down for food."

"Especially after a hard day in the class-room—" He cut off abruptly, almost as though he were afraid that it would up-set her to be reminded that she was no longer a teacher.

"It's okay. I guess I was a little depressed about that today. I... I knew when I quit that I was giving up the privilege of be-ing with the kids and the joy that I get from that. But..." She blew out a breath, digging into her pasta absentminded-ly. "How can I continue to stay there when I'm required to teach things that I completely disagree with, and I'm not allowed to talk about things that are important? Important for life and for eternity. It's like the whole world has gone crazy. Where are the people with brains?"

"I think they probably feel like they have them. But the Bible does say 'professing themselves to be wise, they became fools.' I suppose that's something we should be expecting, instead of being surprised when it happens."

"That's a good point, but I don't have to like it."

"I don't think any of us do. It's a little depressing."

She thought about depressing. Depressing was buying an inn, with the idea that she was going to fix it up, and then realizing that the job was way over her skill set and abilities. Not to mention her financial situation was totally lacking for such a large project.

"I hate it, but I think I'm going to have to put this back up for sale. I will probably lose money on it, but... It was ridiculous in the extreme of me to think that I could fix this up myself."

"Does it have to be an inn?"

Pam froze. The sausage pasta was amazing, so delicious, but she didn't even taste the bite that was still in her mouth as she considered his question. She chewed slowly, swallowing, and then said, "I... I assumed it did."

"There's lots of potential here. I mean, it would be kind of expensive for you to use it as your solo residence, but you could have an assisted care facility, you could foster children, you could open up an afterschool care center for kids. You could do a daycare. You could turn it into a school," he said, the last one uttered almost as though he were reaching for the stars.

But the idea struck her.

She wanted to be a teacher. She hadn't always dreamed of it, but she'd fallen in love with her students. And she didn't want to quit.

"I could. It's... It's almost perfect for that. I mean, the rooms are a little bit small for a classroom, unless you didn't have very many students in your classrooms. They're the perfect size for a small charter school type classroom. Wouldn't that be awesome?" She could get so excited about it, but she tried to keep herself in check because she didn't have any money to fix it up into an inn. She certainly didn't have any money to turn it into a school either.

"Unfortunately, that probably takes just as much, actually more, money than an inn. It wouldn't just be fixing it up, it would be paying teachers, having an administrator, getting the equipment and the electronics and books and whatever you need, and it wouldn't make any money."

"A charter school should make enough to pay the salaries of the teachers anyway, although I don't know that they always have actual buildings. A lot of charter schools are online."

"True. If parents are home to take care of their children. I... I wish I could do it. That's the best idea that I've heard in a long time." She sighed, putting her head back and looking at the ceiling. If only she could get the money from her inheritance. That would be enough to get started anyway.

"Don't you think it's funny sometimes, the way we make our way the way we think God wants us to go?" She looked back out at Lake Michigan, knowing that Mark wasn't going to be able to give her any words of wisdom. He would just commiserate with her.

"You're saying you thought buying the inn was God's will?"

"Yeah. And quitting my job. How could I work in a place where I can't even say the name of Jesus without being threatened with suspension? Unless I'm swearing. I mean, of course I thought it was God's will."

But it was just really what she wanted. Obviously, since she'd gotten herself into a huge mess. She'd spent all her savings on the inn and had very little to live on. If she was careful, she'd be able to live for a year, but she was really counting on getting the inheritance money. She should have asked her mom before she quit her job.

But then...she was back to wondering if she could really continue to work there.

"Maybe God is just pushing you into marriage. Maybe that's what you're supposed to do." Mark lifted his shoulder and took another bite of his food. "This stuff is really good."

His was almost gone, and she'd barely touched hers. Typical man. Could eat during the worst crisis of her life. "Getting married was the biggest mistake I ever made. I don't want to make that mistake again. Plus, there are absolutely zero prospects. And you know that."

"There are plenty of eligible men in town. For a small town, Strawberry Sands has several men who aren't married and are close to your age."

"The only one that I would even consider marrying would be you. And that would be...weird."

Even as she said it, her words were true as she spoke them, but her mind shifted as they hit the air.

Being married to Mark would not be terrible at all. After all, they were already great friends. So what if they had a little piece of paper between them? She wasn't planning on getting married again, and he wasn't either.

"I kind of wish we could. After all, if I were married, my sister wouldn't be shoving her best friend down my throat. She says she doesn't have anywhere else to go, but I kind of feel like she's trying to matchmake us. That's what was going on the last time she stayed, and I think Paulette thinks that I'd forgotten about how she took Bruno to the pound. I have not."

"I can't believe she did that. Bruno was such a sweetheart, and it made the last days of his life so stressful." Pam shuddered. But her mind was still going. "You know, that might not be such a bad idea."

"Taking Bruno to the pound?" Mark almost spit the food out of his mouth. He sputtered.

"No. Getting married. You and me."

That time, the food really did come out.

Chapter 6

Mark choked on his pasta and started coughing, setting his plastic Styrofoam container aside so he didn't spill the rest of it. It was good stuff, but for a couple of scary moments, he thought it might be the death of him. Literally.

And then, he got his airway cleared out enough that he could breathe, and he remembered what had started him choking to begin with.

"You and me?" he managed to say, and then he started coughing again, less because there was something in his throat, and more because those words just...felt so right and so wrong at the same time, he could hardly stand it.

Pam was the perfect woman. Sweet and kind, easygoing and generous, and always willing to lend a hand. She cared about her kids and her job and was honest to a fault. Anytime something broke in her apartment, she told him immediately and paid to have it fixed. He never had to play landlord to her. She took care of everything herself; even the time the toilet had backed up, she called a plumber, and then she helped the plumber while he fixed everything. And paid the bill.

That's part of the reason he never raised her rent. And eventually he told her that the house was paid for and she didn't have to pay him anymore. She just took care of her electric and they split the taxes when they came, and it had been easy.

Pam had been the easiest woman ever.

But he'd never really looked at her as a...wife.

"Do you think we'd be able to stay friends if we got married?"

"It wouldn't really be a real marriage. It would just be a marriage so that I can get my inheritance, and you wouldn't have to put up with Stacy. Of course, you don't have a dog anymore, so there's that."

"Don't forget she killed my plants."

"Oh. Yeah. I forgot about that. Anyway, marrying me would get you out of having to spend the summer with her."

"You know, it shouldn't be as tempting as what it is, but it really is."

"What do you mean it shouldn't be tempting?" she asked, sounding affronted. He thought she was just teasing, but he supposed despite the fact that Pam was pretty much the perfect woman, she still had feminine vanity.

"It's not because you're not appealing in any way, it's just because...we're good friends. I really like you. You don't feel like a wife at all."

"Oh. Yeah, I guess you're not really sup-posed to like your wife."

They snorted together. That seemed to be the way it was so many times. People put up with their significant other, but they didn't really care for them.

He knew a lot of couples like that, although it seemed like the couples in Strawberry Sands actually did love each other. Maybe it was contagious. Al-though if it was, he'd hate to ruin the streak.

"We really wouldn't fit in around town," he said.

"Because all the couples around town seem like they really love each other?"

"Yeah. We'd be the odd couple out."

"Well, even though our local couples seem like they really love each other, they're friends too. We've got that going for us. In fact, several times when we've been at the diner in the summer, tourists have come up and asked us if we were newlyweds, I guess because we were having such a good time together."

"And didn't look like a couple who'd been married for thirty years or anything," he said, irony in his voice. After all, the assumption was that only newlyweds could actually enjoy each other's company. People who had been married for a long time were almost bound to be unhappy as the universal thought went.

He honestly found himself not appalled by the idea of marriage to Pam, which totally surprised him. In fact, he kind of...liked it in a way. Pam was a good friend, and nothing in his life would have to change. They'd just get married, there'd be a piece of paper between them, and they would file joint taxes. Or they could still file separately. The only thing that they'd have to do would be to make sure that they knew who was going to inherit what if one of them died.

"I guess nothing would really have to change," he said thoughtfully, shocked beyond words that he was actually considering this idea.

"Yeah. That's kind of what I was thinking. We'll just...keep things the way they are, and instead of not being married, we'll be married. But nothing needs to change."

"Yeah. That is actually kind of nice. I... I can't really think of a downside."

"Me, either. I mean, you might need to use me as a shield if your sister and Stacy stop in, but that's fine. I would've done it whether we were married or not."

"I know. But putting my best friend in front of me and telling my sister that her friend can't stay is a little bit different than putting my wife in front of me." Mark emphasized the word "wife," and Pam laughed.

"Exactly. It just makes a whole world of difference to everyone else, but it doesn't have to change anything between the two of us."

"I don't think we should rush into any-thing rashly. Let's take a day and think about it, but I'm actually getting excited about the idea. I think this could turn out to be a really beneficial thing, with no downsides. Whenever do you get a chance to do something like that?"

"Exactly."

"But you were just lamenting the idea that you thought something was God's will, and then you did something that you wanted to do instead of what God wanted you to do... Although... Maybe you were wrong. Maybe God really did want you to quit your job, because we probably wouldn't be having this conver-sation if you hadn't."

"We definitely wouldn't have been, and wow. That's an idea. I hadn't considered it at all. Maybe God did want me to make not just one change in my life, but a bunch."

They were quiet for a bit while Mark thought about that. It was funny how one decision could snowball and affect so many other lives, but that seemed to be what was happening, and he had to admit that when he thought about marrying Pam, he didn't get any feeling in his heart but a sense of peace and rightness.

Whether that was because of the way Pam was, whether that was because of the way God was, he wasn't sure. But if he was looking for a peace when making a decision, he definitely had it for this one.

"All right. Let's take a day. We'll think about it, pray about it, and maybe get some advice from some people."

"Who in the world could begin to give advice about that? This is...unprecedented. I'm sure other people have done it, getting married for some kind of convenience, but I don't really know anyone." He tried to think of anyone who had gotten married for anything other than saying that they were in love. It just wasn't done.

But he could kind of see the wisdom in it. Actually, the more he thought about it, the more wisdom he felt was there. Love, such as it was, came and went.

People fell in it, and people fell out of it. But friendship... A friendship especially like the one that Pam and he had, where they'd been friends for more than a decade. Their friendship had weathered a lot of storms, and while they hadn't exactly been living together, they lived side by side and learned to not just like each other but to really care for each other.

He kind of figured that if there was a relationship that could survive a marriage, it would be the one that Pam and he had. He tried hard to think of reasons to not go through with it, but he seriously couldn't think of any other than the fact that it might destroy their friendship. He'd heard of other people saying that once two friends tried to get romantic, their friendship never was the same.

"I think the most important thing is that we just make sure that we stay friends. We don't want to actually try to do anything more than that. That has a tendency to blow up friendships."

"That's what I've heard. I agree with you completely. I've heard that too. And as much as I would love to go through with this, to have the money to be able to rebuild the inn, to see you escape from Stacy, I don't want to lose your friendship over it. That's the most important thing to me."

They nodded to each other, smiling a little, but their eyes were serious. He loved that she was on board with securing their friendship. That it was important to her, and she didn't want to see anything happen to it.

"All right then. We pray about it, and potentially we'll try, but that's the rule. No romance."

She nodded decisively but didn't say anything. He supposed he appreciated that. He didn't want to hear her say that she wasn't the slightest bit romantically interested in him, that he was not attractive, and she knew she wouldn't be tempted in that direction.

He didn't know why that was so disappointing to him. He should wish that she would say it, maybe even prompt her to. Maybe he should have said something like that himself about her, but...it wasn't entirely true. He found himself looking at the curve of Pam's neck, seeing her fingers in his mind as they shaped pie crust in a pan or her cute pink toes as she walked out on the porch in the summer in her bare feet.

He couldn't deny that as a man, the sight stirred him.

But he never acted on those feelings, and while once in a while the idea of kissing Pam had crossed his mind, he never acted on that either. He didn't figure that it would be such a hardship to push those feelings aside and continue as friends. They'd done it for the last ten years, it should be something that they could continue to do for years on end.

Still, he would definitely be praying about this. Marriage was forever. And he didn't want to make a decision like that without making sure that God was in it.

Just the fact that Pam felt the same way gave him peace about the whole situation.

Chapter 7

"Hey," Pam said as she walked out on the front porch. She hadn't expected to see Mark out there, even though in the summer, both of them often spent at least a few minutes every evening out on it, enjoying the small-town atmosphere and the warm weather.

It had been unseasonably warm for May, and it was still early in the season.

She just...thought better on the front porch, she supposed. Or maybe she needed a break from her thoughts. The idea of marrying Mark. It was crazy, it was exciting. It was the wildest idea she'd ever had, and at the same time, there was no doubt that she felt total and complete confidence that if they did it, it would work out.

"Hey. I guess this is our thinking spot," he joked, sliding over a bit so she could sit down on the top of the steps with him.

She sat down the way she always did, but it was funny how she was suddenly aware of him beside her. Of the strength of his leg and the way his forearm rested on it. His breath. Things she never thought about at all were suddenly filling up her senses.

He smelled like soap and cleanliness, with a strength underlying it all that was very familiar to her, yet she'd never really examined.

"Looks like Luke and Kristin are going to come over and say hi to us."

That was one of the reasons why she often went outside on the porch. Sometimes she walked across the road and said hi to her neighbors, and sometimes other folks out for an evening stroll stopped in. Sometimes tourists stopped to chat.

It felt like she was part of the small town when she was out on her porch.

"I think you're right," she said as she watched Luke and Kristin, their hands joined together, walk across the road and step up on the sidewalk.

"Good evening. It's beautiful out for early May," Luke said by way of greeting.

"I guess I shouldn't have been surprised everyone else was out, but it does seem like it's early in the year for us all to be acting like it's summer," Mark replied.

Pam greeted Kristin and invited them to sit down.

Luke sat on the step beside them, and Kristin sat on the step below his, settling between his legs and leaning against his chest. His arms came around her, and they looked so cozy and sweet it made Pam's heart squeeze.

That's what she would be giving up. She hadn't really thought about it, hadn't realized it until just now, but she always held out a little bit of hope in her heart that maybe someday she'd have a relationship like that. Where she cuddled easily with her husband. Where they held hands and touched and snuggled and shared secret special smiles.

She tried to shake those thoughts. After all, what she had with Mark was even better. They laughed together, they understood each other, and they supported each other. They knew each other's bad habits and character flaws, and they enjoyed each other's company anyway. She would even say that she loved Mark. As friends. Even though she knew he wasn't a perfect man.

She felt something and looked down. Mark had touched her arm, and her eyes caught on his finger, long and capable, and somehow just looking at it made...some kind of feeling radiate out from her chest. She couldn't define it, and its intensity surprised her.

She jerked her eyes up to his. He had his brows raised in question.

It took her a minute to yank her thoughts away from the feeling in her body to what question he might be asking her.

She realized he must want to talk to Kristin and Luke and ask their advice.

With a small smile, she nodded her head toward Kristin and Luke and then looked back at him.

He nodded with a grin, that grin saying that he knew she would understand what he was asking, and it was just a shared knowledge that passed between them. The way it felt when she knew someone so well that they talked without words.

She loved that feeling and realized that she did it quite often with Mark.

"So, to be too personal, but I'm thinking about making a pretty big life change and can't help but notice that you and Kristin seem to be friends, as well as husband and wife. I'm just wondering how you accomplish that."

"That's an odd question," Luke said, his words a little dry, and Pam got the feeling that he could see right through what Mark was asking.

"Oh my goodness, you and Pam are thinking about getting married! And you worry that it's going to ruin your friendship." Kristin's smile went up like two hundred million times. "I think that is awesome. And I think that marriages based on friendship like the one you and Pam have, which is super strong—I've often admired it—are the best marriages. After all, if you're friends before you're married, you just become better friends afterward."

"It's not automatic though," Luke said, looking down at Kristin as she tilted her head and looked up at him, grinning.

"It is for you, but for me, you're right. I had to work on it a little."

He snorted. "You can see what I put up with here," he said, talking to Pam and Mark and grinning at them.

Kristin reached her hand around and squeezed his neck while he put his head down and pressed his lips to her temple.

It was so sweet and cute that it made Pam's heart squeeze again.

She wanted to look over at Mark and see what he was thinking about all of that, but she didn't want to at the same time. She supposed she was afraid.

She wasn't going to allow fear to dictate her life, so she straightened her shoulders and turned her head.

Mark noticed her movement, and his head turned and their eyes met.

She couldn't read the expression on his face. Maybe it was because dusk was falling, or maybe it was because there wasn't an expression there, at least not one that she recognized.

They really didn't talk about romantic things at all.

Nothing besides her failed marriage, which was so far from romance, it wasn't even funny.

"Seriously, guys. You should go for it. Getting married was the best decision I ever made."

"You think you're going to feel that way in ten years?" Mark asked with a wisdom that surprised Pam. She hadn't considered it, but it was true. Sometimes newness wore off, and what started out as something wonderful turned into something that was a ball and chain. But how could one project that far into the future? How could one think that it might change? Obviously, if they felt that it would go that way, they wouldn't have gotten married to begin with, right?

"That's a good question. I guess you have to ask me in ten years, because right now, I say no."

"I'd say that in order for it to not, we have to make a conscious decision to make sure that it doesn't. A marriage isn't something that just flourishes without care. You have to put the time and effort into it."

"People always say that, but I don't understand what time and effort they're talking about."

"The same kind of time and effort you put into a relationship when you're dating. You try to win someone, then you get married, and they don't feel special and new anymore, and you feel like you don't have to do things for them like you used to. But it's like getting out of bed whenever she hears a noise. I want to roll over and go back to sleep, because I know it's nothing, but that's just dismissing her thoughts and her concerns. I wouldn't dismiss anything she said if we were dating. So why do I think it's okay to do whenever we get married? That's the kind of time and effort you have to put into a relationship. The kind of time and effort that is doing things that are inconvenient for you. Just because they make her happy."

"All you have to do is smile at me and you make me happy."

"All right. Next time you hear a noise in the middle of the night, I won't get up, I'll just smile at you. We'll see how that works."

"Okay. You're right."

"That's another thing. Sometimes you just have to give in. I mean, some of us are right more than others..."

"Ouch," he said as Kristin playfully smacked his head.

"I know what you are insinuating, and I just want to make sure that they understand that it was actually the opposite of what you said."

"All right. She's right at least, oh, forty percent of the time."

"Luke?"

"Forty-one percent?"

"We can finish this argument later," she said, and Pam felt her cheeks heating.

"There you go. There's something else. You can't take your arguments too seriously. And you have to be willing to make up. Someone has to be humble."

He gave a long-suffering sigh. "Ask how I know."

"Would you stop? They're going to think I'm a monster."

"We're not going to think any such thing. You guys are adorable," Pam interrupted. It was fun to listen to them banter back and forth, and it was sweet to know that they had so much fun together.

That was the kind of marriage she wanted. Where she and her husband laughed about things. Where they didn't get offended over everything, where they appreciated each other, where they...enjoyed spending time with each other and chose to be with each other, even when they didn't have to be. After all, right now, Luke could be sitting in front of the

TV or doing some other manly pursuit, while Kristin did something in a completely different part of the house. But they'd made the decision for each of them to give up what maybe they wanted to do and to spend time together.

She assumed that each of them preferred to spend time with the other, rather than doing whatever it was that they could be doing.

She wasn't sure whether her brain was reasoning that out, but she felt like she knew what she was talking about.

Where they had a choice of a whole bunch of different things that they could do, and they chose to spend time together, because that's what they really wanted. To be with each other, over everything else.

But she couldn't control that. She couldn't make her husband want her. Couldn't make him want to spend time with her or even want to banter and laugh and joke. She couldn't make him not get upset, and she couldn't make him look at her and think she was the most wonderful woman in the world, even when she wasn't.

It was discouraging. She couldn't imagine anyone looking at her like that. She had so many faults and flaws, she certainly wasn't beautiful, even when she was younger, and now that she was in her fifties, she wouldn't be gracing the cover of any magazines, anywhere, ever.

Whereas Mark, it was unfair, but it seemed like men got better as they aged. He had the salt-and-pepper hair that made him look distinguished rather than old, and while he wasn't beanpole thin, the little bit of pouch that he had made him look more approachable, almost teddy bear status, like he was not quite perfect and therefore immensely lovable.

Did she want to be with someone who other women would be admiring and trying to catch his eye? Especially maybe they would be looking at her and wondering what someone like him was doing with her. And he would wonder the same thing. She really didn't want that.

"So when's the big day?" Luke asked, interrupting her thoughts.

"I don't know. We haven't decided." Mark sounded surprised, like they hadn't thought about it at all, which was the absolute truth.

"We were thinking about doing it quickly though. No big fanfare. We're both in our fifties, and it seems kind of silly to have a big celebration at this point in our lives."

"I've heard a lot of people say they wish they had the money back they spent on their wedding. But it's not every day that you get married, and it is nice to mark the occasion." Kristin spoke, her hands on Luke's knee. "Our wedding wasn't super big. And I don't regret that at all."

"I guess we'll talk about it. But I agree with Pam. If she's okay with something small, that would be my preference as well. I think, less than the wedding, the marriage should take priority. Figuring out how to make it something that rep-resents Christ and the church, and not be something that we just endure."

Pam felt her stomach flutter, like a whole nest of butterflies had erupted in it.

He was saying the words she really want-ed to hear. Maybe that they were going to push the wedding under the rug, but they were going to work to make sure that it was something that they were both happy in. She liked that a lot better than just getting married and then ignoring it.

But...was that crossing the line of romance? She didn't want to do that, because she really did agree with Luke about that, too. It would ruin their relationship if everything went south. She didn't want to end up regretting this marriage as much as she regretted her first marriage.

They chatted some more with Luke and Kristin before one of their daughters came out and started calling for them.

"We're being paged," Luke said as Kristin stood up, and he stood up behind her.

"I don't know if this is something that you're talking to everyone about, but we'll keep it under our hats if you want us to," Luke said as they stretched and began making their way down the steps.

"If you would. That'd be great. We… We still haven't made any definite plans," Mark said, and Pam appreciated it. She didn't want to have to deal with questions in town if they decided not to go through with it.

But she'd had more than twenty-four hours to think about it, and she really felt totally at peace.

Kristin and Luke walked off, and she and Mark sat in silence for a little bit.

"So I don't know what you've been thinking, but I've been praying about this, thinking about it, and Luke isn't the first person I asked something along those lines. I… I can't believe what a peace I have about it. But I said to myself that I wasn't going to push you. If you have any doubts at all, I don't think we should do it."

"I actually can't wait. I was really hoping you would come to the same conclusion. Because I thought the same thing. I wasn't going to push you into it. But I have no doubts at all."

She had a little bit of a longing for romance, should she admit that?

Like he could tell there was something bothering her, he asked, "Is there anything at all that you feel might be an issue?"

"I guess I was watching Luke and Kristin, and I love the way they act together. I've always wanted that. And that's the only negative feeling I had. That, if we do this, I guess I'm giving that up. The idea of having someone to cuddle with, someone to share those secret smiles and laughter that only lovers do. You know?"

She and Mark hardly ever talked about anything like that. Their relationship just didn't include romance at all.

"You know, it's funny, I wouldn't admit this to just anyone, but I was feeling the same thing. I believe what I told you yesterday about romance ruining friendships, but maybe... Maybe after we've been married for a little bit, it could be something that we can talk about again?"

"That's taking a bit of a chance, but it's only a small chance in my opinion, and it's totally worth it."

"I guess I have to agree with you there. You can't really make a decision and think that there's only positives associated with that decision. This is just something that we're going to have to chance. Honestly, I'm comfortable with you."

She hadn't realized it, but he had moved a little bit closer, and after he said that, he put his hand on her shoulder.

It felt different. He'd never really touched her before. Not on purpose, not...as anything more than a friend. Maybe this wasn't that, but it felt a little bit more intimate. Anytime they'd been on the porch in the dark, they hadn't sat close enough that they could even hold hands. And there he was touching her.

She considered her options. Then, holding her breath, feeling her heart beat hard and swift in her chest, she lifted her hand and moved slowly until it settled lightly down on his leg.

It was hard, warm, and it felt solid and strong under her fingers.

She didn't allow her fingers to move, but they wanted to.

She held her breath and waited for him to speak. For her, yeah. This definitely was okay.

"I think we might be making the right decision." That was all he said, and she wasn't entirely sure of what exactly that meant, other than he was okay with it too. Whether he liked it, whether he thought that there could be something more than friendship in their relationship, she wasn't sure.

"All right then. I'm ready to do it if you are." She couldn't help it, her fingers tightened just a little on his leg, and his breath hitched.

She wasn't sure why, but that sound made it so that her heart hammered even faster, and her own lungs felt like they couldn't get enough air.

Maybe, maybe this was going to work out after all.

"I'm pretty sure that was the shortest wedding ceremony ever," Mark said, laughing to himself at how crazy the morning had been.

"It's kind of funny our pastor got called away to be at the bedside of a family member, and he had a friend come up to do it. But then he got called away too."

"Thankfully he married us before he left. Or we'd still be wandering around trying to figure out what to do, where we could find a preacher, or if our wedding day wasn't actually going to be our wedding day."

"It was a crazy day all right. I suppose it'll be memorable just because of the brevity. I'm pretty sure he missed about half of the vows."

"I said them in my head."

Normally she would have laughed at that remark, but there was a serious note in Mark's voice that made her think that maybe he actually did mean that.

"I did too," she said, and that was true.

"I think the important thing is that you agree to obey me. As long as you said that one, then we're good."

"Whoops. I forgot that one." She grinned.

"That's it. I need to go get my money back. I got cheated."

"I'm pretty sure I paid, because someone forgot his wallet."

"Oh. Forgot that too. But that's okay, because I'm buying supper."

"That's awesome. You mean I don't have to cook on my wedding day?"

"I heard that Griff was making his smoky kicky Italian sausage pasta again, and it seems like we have that on all the important occasions in our relationship—"

"We had it once."

"Well, it was the day that we first thought about getting married. That's pretty much all the important occasions in our relationship, right?"

"I'm pretty sure that we had other important times."

"In our friendship. But this is more important than friendship. This is...a relationship."

She laughed outright. He said it like
there was a difference. Like he was going to explain to her what a relationship
was.

"You know what, I think that this conversation is going to be way too frustrat-
ing for me to continue with. Especially
if you're going to explain to me what a
relationship is."

"I'm offended."

"I think as long as you get food in your stomach, you'll forget that you're offended."

"And I think you know me a little too well."

"However, you did say that we would spend the rest of the day researching people who might be donors for the school and trying to figure out who in the world we need to contact in order for us to move forward with the building. We're going to need an architect, and I think it might be a good idea to just hire a firm who does everything. It's such a huge project. It might be really hard to piecemeal it together."

"I'm in total agreement with that. I'm also going to have to call my sister. I'd like to announce the news of our happy nuptials, so I don't get unpleasantly surprised by a visit and a visitor."

She laughed. "I suppose I should call my mom."

He pulled into the drive on the opposite side that she was used to. There hadn't been too many occasions where she and Mark had driven around together, and this was something that she was going to have to get used to.

"All right then, we'll spend a few hours working, and then we'll take a break and eat, and make our phone calls."

The afternoon went by quickly. She had to admit that Mark made everything more fun. Even research. They found several firms that would be able to do exactly what they needed them to, and two of them promised to come out and look at the property and give them quotes.

They came up with a long list of donors as well, and then, after looking at each other since neither one of them was looking forward to doing it, they split the list in half, and each of them started making phone calls.

It was discouraging at first, since her first three phone calls produced absolutely nothing, but then she called a doctor from Blueberry Beach. Dr. John. He pledged a large amount of money.

That made things feel real. And it also made her start to think about taxes and setting up some type of financial windfall, and they spent an hour on the phone talking to an accountant before they made an appointment for the next week.

Two hours later, they had more than three million dollars pledged.

"I don't know why I was resistant to that idea to begin with, but it was brilliant," Pam said.

Mark volunteered to go get food while she finished up and called her mom.

She figured she might as well get the call out of the way, and then they could truly relax for the rest of the day. Maybe it wasn't what people traditionally did on their wedding day, but she felt like it had been one of the best days of her life.

Her idyllic life of being a schoolteacher had blown up not that long ago, but it was tantalizingly close now, and she had Mark to thank for it.

Of course, she put work in it too, but if he hadn't come up with the idea, she'd still be depressed and thinking about her students and wondering if she had done the right thing.

Thank you, Lord. It feels so good to move forward and to know that this whole thing has been orchestrated by You.

Even down to their marriage. Which was crazy. No one got married the way they did. But no one parted the waters of the sea and allowed a million people to walk through on dry ground, either. No one allowed His son to be crucified so that all of mankind could be saved. God was a God of doing things that no one else thought to do.

It was kind of fun to serve a God like that. A girl never knew what He was going to have in store next for her.

She smiled, smiled at the peace in her soul and how she felt light and not just weightless, but bright, like when God was around, the darkness disappeared.

She wished she could hold that feeling close, but she had a feeling that it was going to go away as she picked up her phone, took a breath, and dialed her mother's number.

"Pamela, two calls in the same week. I feel like maybe you missed me."

"I just wanted to let you know that I got married. I thought you'd be happy for me, and excited."

She didn't figure there was any point in beating around the bush. Sometimes her mom could be brief, and if she thought that she was just calling to chitchat, she would rush off. Pam didn't want to get off the phone without telling her her news. It was hard enough to pick up the phone and make the first call. She didn't want to have to struggle to do it again.

"You got married."

"I sure did."

"To who? And why didn't I meet him? And why did I not even know about this?"

"Well, first of all, Mom, you have met him. It's Mark, my neighbor. And I did kind of warn you. I called you last week."

"You called me last week to ask about your inheritance and to try to get me to give it to you without you getting married."

"Well, maybe Mark and I wanted to wait a little bit, but we also want to get started on a project, and the money will definitely come in handy."

"I'm sure it will. Five million dollars comes in handy to a lot of people." Her mother's tone dripped with disbelief. "He must've married you for your money." She made a tsking sound, and then she said, "I don't believe he really cares for you." She sighed. "I'm going to have to make a trip there. Get my room ready, I'll be there tomorrow."

Her mother hung up.

Well, that wasn't what she was expecting.

Now her mother was coming, and they'd made plans to meet with one of the building firms and an accountant next week... She got married, and all of a sudden, her social calendar had filled up.

She wanted to laugh, but that was probably just a stress relief. After all, she was going to have to tell Mark when he came back with the food that her mother was coming to make sure that he didn't marry her for her money.

She dreaded that, because not only that, she had to tell him that her mother was going to visit. And she would be watching to see that Mark and she had an actual marriage.

She hadn't considered that they might actually have to pass a test like that. With someone staying in their house.

By the time he got home, she was pacing the floor.

"Uh oh. The call with your mother didn't go very well."

"No. It didn't."

He narrowed his eyes, as though trying to figure out what might have gone wrong, as he walked in the door to her side of the duplex and carried the food to the table.

She set it with silverware and poured them each a glass of water.

The kitchen was bright and cheery, facing the southern sky so lots of sunlight came in no matter the time of year. Currently, it was brightly lit, and the light in the room chased away some of the darkness in her heart. Mark was not going to like her news, but he was not the kind of man who got angry or unreasonable. They would figure this out. Together.

"Well, I didn't have the best conversation with my sister either. She's coming anyway. Gonna be here tomorrow."

"You're kidding," she said, laughing despite herself. "She probably will arrive at exactly the same time as my mom, who is also coming tomorrow since she's determined that you have married me for my money, and she's going to come and check up on us. I don't know what she's going to do if she decides that that's what happened, but... Hopefully it's not keep my money from me."

"I don't think she can do that."

"Well, she's managed to do it since my aunt died. I was supposed to inherit without any conditions, but Mom said I had to get married. So far, I haven't fought her on it. It would require hiring a lawyer, and I just didn't want to do that."

"I don't blame you. I wouldn't want to hire a lawyer against my own mother either. That would make a bad relation-ship…"

"…disintegrate," she filled in for him, unable to think of a worse word. Because, whatever the worse word was, was what was going to happen.

"All right. We can handle this. It's our first test as a married couple, and we're going to do just fine."

"Plus, as I was walking across the street, Bill and Bev from Blueberry Beach called me back. They didn't answer the phone the first time I called. They pledged one million dollars. Told me to let them know when I had things set up, and he'd cut me a check that day."

"You're kidding!" she said, her eyes getting bright and her whole body feeling like the heaviness that had settled down when she talked to her mom had lifted.

"Nope. Best news we've had all day, isn't it?"

"It's certainly better news than having my mom coming."

"Or my sister. Or Stacy."

They laughed, and he pulled the containers out of the bag.

"We can develop a game plan. I mean, after all, we're going to have to stick together if we're going to outsmart your mom. She is...one of a kind."

"That's probably the nicest thing someone could say about her," Pam said, knowing that he could have found a lot of different words to use, and he'd chosen to be kind. She appreciated that. Even though her mom tried every nerve in her body and often twisted the very last one to the snapping point, she still loved her. She was still her mom. Her family. And she felt a little defensive whenever anyone else tried to insult or belittle her.

Mark knew that, had heard her explain that she didn't understand it, even though it was true. She appreciated the fact that he wasn't railing against her.

"So we're going to have to...look like we're in love, I guess."

"Yeah. Although we don't want to go overboard. I called her last week to ask about the money."

"I remember."

"And I hadn't said that I was madly in love with anyone or planning on getting married. So, I think that she'll believe us if we're just honest about what happened. You know, we're good friends, and our relationship has been a long time coming."

"Well, ten years is a long time. That's for sure."

Her phone rang, and it took her a second as she looked at the screen to realize it was the third company that they called for estimates on giving them a design that would work for their vision in the end.

"Do you want me to get it now?" she asked after she explained who it was, not wanting to talk on the phone while they were eating but not wanting to miss the call either.

Mark must have felt the same way, because he nodded his head. "Sure. Grab it. We weren't able to get a hold of them, and it'd be really nice to have three estimates to choose from."

"I agree."

She answered the phone, and thoughts of her mom faded away as she talked to the person on the other end. They were very accommodating, and they actually even sounded excited about the project. Plus, they were the most local group, having their home base in Blueberry Beach. When they had been talking about which companies to use, this was the company she most wanted.

By the time she got off the phone, she was hoping and praying that this was the company that they would end up going with. Since she had the phone on speaker, Mark had heard the entire conversation, and he didn't have to say anything for her to look at his sparkling eyes and know that he felt the exact same way that she did.

Maybe it was an unconventional wedding day, but they didn't have a problem finding things to talk about, ideas to share, and even the specter of her mother visiting the next day didn't discourage them.

Maybe they hadn't had a big wedding, but she couldn't have imagined a better wedding day.

Chapter 9

"What's wrong?" Pam asked as she walked into Mark's kitchen.

Through the years, they'd developed a routine. In the winter, he did most of the cooking, since she taught school and she was always knee-deep in correcting homework and directing plays and whatever else she managed to get herself involved in. And in the summer, she did most of the cooking since that's when his job as landscaper was the most busy. Sometimes he left before dark and came home after, and considering how long the Michigan summer days were, that was a lot of time away.

In the summer and fall, they seemed to play it by ear. Whoever got up first did breakfast. Sometimes they planned it and even talked about it, and sometimes it was just whoever got up or whoever managed to cook.

Today, Pam had gotten up and moseyed over to Mark's house, but while he was usually relaxed and pretty chill, today he was rushing around his kitchen, grabbing some things and throwing them in his lunch box and looking rather frazzled.

"I bid on a job a month ago, and I kind of forgot about it. I way overbid it because I didn't really need the work, and honestly, I wasn't expecting to get it."

"But you got it," she deduced.

He stopped, thermos in one hand, coffeepot in the other. "Exactly. I'm sorry."

Her eyes widened. "It's okay."

"Well, I know our marriage wasn't real or anything, but it was just yesterday, and... I don't know, I feel like I'm rushing out the door today, and maybe you were expecting to... I don't know."

"Have a honeymoon?" she asked, laughter making the sides of her mouth turn up.

"No. I guess not. I just... I just feel a little bit bad."

"Don't feel bad. What are you doing, exactly? I've helped you before."

He had poured the coffee into the thermos, and now he set the thermos down on the counter slowly like he was thinking. "Really? Because you could. It's a tree-planting job about ten miles up the beach. They are trying to reforest an area that was timbered off this past winter."

"That's a little out of your normal area of expertise."

"I know. But these jobs always pay crazy money. And they're really not that hard."

"Just takes manpower."

"Exactly. I have Chip and Stan, but I could really use you too. I wasn't sure I was going to be able to get it done today, but with you, I know I can." He gave her an engaging grin, and she was glad that she volunteered.

Even though she had a ton of work that she could be doing at the inn, there wasn't any great time crunch on that. And she enjoyed spending time with Mark. He always made things fun, and it made her feel good to help him. He'd been such a huge help to her over the years, with her girls, with the issues that she was having with school, and now, marrying her to help her get her inher-itance.

"I owe you."

His nose wrinkled up as he dug another thermos out of his cupboard. "I don't like to hear that. I don't feel like you do."

"After yesterday." She went to his refrigerator and pulled the creamer out; he always bought the caramel creamer she loved, and she also pulled the plain creamer out for him.

"That should help me just as much as it helps you. If I don't have to put up with Stacy this summer, it will be a huge benefit. I think what I'd owe you would actually be worth more than however much money you're inheriting from your mom."

"I suppose you could be right. With all that Stacy did the last time, I can't believe your sister's even thinking that you would be interested in having her again."

They'd already talked about that, but it just was one of those things that Pam figured she'd never understand.

She poured caramel creamer into the thermos that he just filled up before she put a few drops of the regular creamer in his.

He hated cold coffee, and while he enjoyed creamer, he never put much in because it made his coffee too cold.

He threw two spoonfuls of sugar into her coffee and then screwed the lid on while she put the creamer back in the refrigerator.

"My sister's pretty determined. I think she sees Stacy and I getting together, and thankfully what you and I did yesterday will put a big wrench into those plans. Because Stacy and I were never getting together." He spoke as he closed the doors to his cupboards and reached up to grab the bread from the back of his counter.

She opened the refrigerator door and grabbed the mayonnaise and mustard that sat on the shelf. "I'm actually glad that we're doing this. I laid awake last night thinking about the inn and trying to figure out what in the world I can do. I mean, the money issues are almost out of my mind. Although, knowing my mom, she'll find a way not to give it to me."

"I know you don't want to hire a lawyer—"

"No. I can't sue my mom."

They talked about that a lot before. Mark had gently nudged her in that direction, but she absolutely refused. She would rather not have the money than have a lawsuit among family members.

He pulled two pieces of bread out of the bag and held them in his hand while he turned to look at her. "You know, I really admire you for that."

"I thought I was just really dumb," she said, setting the mustard and mayonnaise down and grabbing a knife from the drawer.

"No. You believe that God wants you to get along with people. I mean, I think all Christians believe that. But we also want to say to ourselves that God doesn't want us to be a doormat. But you can't find that verse in the Bible."

"I know. I think that's more about pride than anything. But it definitely appeals to our human nature."

"It appeals to mine. I don't want people walking all over me. And I want to make sure I get what's coming to me. I think everybody does."

"I do." She sure did. She'd been upset at her mom more than once. But her mom had been resistant, and Pam just couldn't hire a lawyer and go through the legal channels that she knew were available to her to get the money. As much as it pained her for her mom to continue to keep it.

"And it amazes me how you're always thinking the best about her."

"Well, that's another command."

"I know. But it's a command that we don't follow. Like, I want to think that she's spent the money secretly, or doesn't want you to have it, or is just being manipulative. But you always say that she cares about you, and you say she thinks she's doing the right thing, actually thinks she's helping you by not giving you the money. I just... I love how you always look at things in a positive manner. No matter how obvious it might be to the rest of the world that it couldn't possibly be the real reason she's not giving you the money."

"I think if I find out that it's something else, I'll have a real hard time continuing to have a relationship with her, you know?"

"I know. But also, you do it because you know it's the right thing to do."

She put mustard on her sandwich and mayonnaise on his two sandwiches while he grabbed the meat and folded it onto the bread.

"I think that's why God gave us the command. Don't you? He wants us to have relationships. I think that teaching is the basis for Christianity. It's about relationships. About other people. And it's interesting to me how studies have shown that the more relationships you have, or maybe the better and stronger your relationships, the healthier you tend to be. I don't think that's a coincidence that God, who made us and who wrote the owner's manual, knows exactly what's going to make us healthy. Good, strong, happy relationships. And sometimes that means giving up what we think our 'rights' are."

"Giving up millions of dollars in order to have a relationship. Now that's someone who puts their convictions into practice. I admire that."

She grinned at him. He didn't typically say things like that, and maybe he really was feeling bad that they just got married yesterday, and there hadn't been any kind of celebration about it.

Not that she wanted one. It wasn't supposed to be a real marriage. So why would they celebrate it like it was?

But she had to admit, she appreciated the fact that he wanted to do something special for her. It made him feel like a real friend. After all, friends celebrated things with other friends.

She put the condiments back in the refrigerator and pulled out the cheese.

She wasn't as young as she used to be, and she knew it was going to be a hard day. Planting trees wasn't difficult work, but by the end of the day, her back and legs would be sore, and tomorrow would be even worse.

"It stinks to get old." She tried not to complain about it too much. After all, with her increased years came increased wisdom. Maybe not as much wisdom as she'd like to have, but more than she used to anyway.

"Don't be silly. You're not old." He nudged her with his shoulder as he walked by her to grab the baggies while she put cheese on their sandwiches, two slices for hers, one for his.

"I appreciate you trying to make me feel better, and I hate to break it to you, but you're getting old too."

"Being old is a state of mind. And fifty is the new twenty."

"Says no one, ever."

"All right. You can officially say you got me depressed. Since one of the reasons I overbid on this job was because I knew that after a day of planting trees, my back, legs, shoulders, hips, and pretty much everything in my body was going to hurt. Worse than it normally does. Since they pretty much hurt all day every day anyway."

"That's more like it. I want to complain a little. You were being all Pollyanna on me."

"Pollyanna accusing me of being Pollyanna. That's rich." He rolled his eyes as he walked by her. She smacked him on the head as she grabbed the cheese and walked to the refrigerator to put it away.

She grabbed the ice packs out of the freezer, one for each lunch box, and walked back over to the counter. "Seriously, being a landscaper is a physical job. Are you going to keep trying to do it until you retire?"

"Being the owner of the company gives me a few perks, but it's hard for me to imagine sitting behind a desk all day while all my employees go out and do the jobs. I... I don't really look forward to that. But I suppose the day is coming."

"I suppose it is." She didn't say anything else. She worried about him occasionally, since he did have such a physical job, and it wasn't something that was typically easy for people their age.

"Good help is hard to find, and I don't know if I'll ever be able to find enough employees to work so that I don't have to. It's a hassle."

She hadn't meant to open up that can of worms either. They'd talked about it more than once. Because landscaping was a seasonal job, it was difficult to find people who could work year after year. A lot of times, he had to start with brand-new employees every year.

And on jobs like this one, ones that had to be done before kids were out of school, he often had trouble finding anyone to help him at all.

"It's a good thing you have a next-door neighbor who is no longer employed."

He smiled at her joke as he shoved the sandwiches in the baggies.

She set the ice packs down in the bottom of the lunch boxes, then went to the cupboard where he always kept a stash of potato chips and crackers.

Being in Mark's kitchen was like being in her own. It felt familiar and safe. Thoughts of getting old were a little scary. She didn't want to have pain every day or not be able to do the things she wanted to do. While she wouldn't trade the wisdom for anything, it felt like a steep price to pay.

Of course, now that she was married, the future didn't stretch out so dark and dreary with her by herself. Except, what did their marriage mean? Did it change anything at all? It didn't feel like anything had changed. In fact, for a while there, she'd forgotten that they'd even gotten married.

Everything felt...the way it always had.

She considered that throughout the day as they drove to the job and then worked for hours on end planting trees.

Chip and Stan worked on the other small patch, while Mark and she did the larger one.

It probably would have worked out better for Mark to put himself with Chip and her with Stan, but she appreciated the fact that she got to work with him.

Maybe he did it so he could look out for her. She wanted to believe that, and it would be in character for Mark. He was always trying to do considerate things that would make her life easier. That was just the kind of guy he was.

By the end of the day, she wasn't thinking anything but about how hungry she was, which was overshadowed only by her thinking about how sore her back was, not to mention her hands, her hips, and pretty much every body part she had.

Chip and Stan finished and left before they did, and Mark walked over to inspect their work. It wasn't terrible, and he nodded in satisfaction before he turned around and walked back to his pickup. Slowly, limping a little.

"How do you feel about supper at the diner?" he asked.

"I feel real good about that. But I think I'd like to go home and take a shower first."

"Yeah, and at least change clothes. It was a lot wetter here than what I thought it was going to be, and I feel like I have mud caked everywhere."

"This time of year, everything's muddy." Although living along the beach, and that close to Lake Michigan, there was a lot of sand in their soil, and it didn't cake the way soil had. That made sense since they were currently higher, more on a cliff above the lake, and wooded to the very edge of the cliff.

It was a beautiful spot, wild and with a great view of the lake, but at this point, she was ready to sit down for a while. She didn't care whether she had a cushion or not, as long as she didn't have to hold a shovel.

Chapter 10

"All right. I've got my quota of planting trees in for the next decade," Pam said with a weary sigh.

"I think in another decade, I'm definitely done planting trees." Mark grinned.

"Seriously? After today, you're still thinking you got another ten years of this in you?" Even though he was several years deeper into his fifties than what she was, she had been thinking that she never wanted to do it again.

"Sure. I guess... I guess I'm just too stubborn to admit that maybe I should leave this for the young kids and go get myself a desk job."

She shook her head. She'd known that Mark always enjoyed being outside. And she had to admire the way he loved his job, and his love of the great outdoors, and his need for the feeling of freedom. Because, with all the pain she had experienced today, and the way she felt so exhausted, she would happily give up being outside in order to not feel this terrible again.

No matter how many times she told herself that suffering made her stronger, she just couldn't imagine voluntarily putting herself through this, except she had. For Mark.

She wasn't sure what that said about her.

They were just ten minutes away from Strawberry Sands when her phone buzzed.

"It's a text from my mom," she said as she lifted it up to look at it.

> **I'm coming to see you tonight. Don't eat supper, I'll take you to the diner. Do they have anything good?**

She read it out loud.

Mark snorted. "If you hadn't told me that was from your mother, I could've guessed."

They laughed together.

"She is a little bossy, isn't she?"

"You did not get that from her. Are you sure you weren't switched at the hospital?"

"I've asked myself that more than once over the years." She flipped the phone over in her hand, trying to figure out what to say. She did not feel like dealing with her mom tonight.

"You look too much like her to not be her daughter. But you must act like your father."

"I hope not. He didn't stick around to raise his kids. I don't want to be like him in anything."

"Yeah." Mark's tone was subdued.

"I wasn't yelling at you. I'm sorry. I just... I don't know, I want to be different from both my parents. Even though I love my mom, she's not my role model."

"You have a healthy way of looking at it. I think sometimes we don't just not want to be like them, we don't want to be with them at all. And you always make time for her. I know you're trying to figure out how to do that tonight."

"I'm exhausted."

"You're also married."

"Oh." She totally forgot about that. "Um, can I say thank you for reminding me?" she said with a smile across the seat at him. She had just about been ready to make a big blunder and not ask Mark what he wanted and also tell her mom that she was too tired to eat and she was going straight to bed or something.

"I guess… I guess if you don't mind, we'll have to show up together." She hadn't considered any of this. She supposed she thought they just had time, and they would figure things out. "Do we live at my side of the duplex or yours?"

"Mine. The woman always moves in with the man." He said that in a pseudo-macho voice, so she knew he was joking.

"All right. Is that what you prefer, truly?"

"I guess I don't care, but if your mom's gonna stay with you, I suppose I'd rather you and I be sleeping on the other side of a solid wall."

She laughed. "You know, that's how I know you actually like me. Because you put up with my mother over the years."

"It's been a trial. Although, she does have her moments. I wonder if she was treating both of us to dinner at the diner?"

"I'm going to assume that she was. After all, she knows I'm married now. It's a two for one at this point."

"All right. I guess I shouldn't be nervous. But there is a part of me that's concerned that I'm going to do something that's going to tip her off and you'll end up not getting your inheritance."

"After you made a lifetime vow to me just so that you could help me get it, I would never in a million years believe that you would do something to try to keep me from it. Not on purpose anyway. And if that happens, I'm just going to assume that it wasn't meant to be." Although, she didn't want to think that God would not want her to inherit the five million that her aunt had left her in her will, but if He threw yet another wrench into the plans, she'd be forced to consider that that was what He actually wanted.

"I guess God couldn't be more clear, if I go through all this trouble to try to get what is rightfully mine, and He still doesn't let me have it."

"And you wouldn't be mad about that?" Mark asked as he pulled into the drive.

"No. I mean, I'll be bitterly disappointed. But God is still in charge, and I have to submit to Him."

Her mom's car wasn't in the drive yet, and she breathed a sigh of relief

"All right. It's good to know that you're human at least. Sometimes, sometimes I just don't understand how you can be so chill about things."

"That's funny. Out of the two of us, I think anyone who's looking at us would call you the most chill."

"You know what I mean."

"I think it has to do with just allowing God to be in charge. I have to admit that He knows better than I do, and for me to try to micromanage what He already has under control is pointless. Sometimes I don't remember that. You know I'm not always chill."

"You're the most chill person I know. And by chill, I mean content to allow God to run your life. I... I sometimes wish I could do that as well as you do it."

"There are a lot of things I wish I could do as well as you. Like planting trees. I'm not sure I can get out of this truck. My body has stiffened up to the point where blinking my eyes hurts."

"But talking doesn't?" He gave her a lop-sided grin as he jerked the handle of his door. "Hold on a second. I'll come over and give you a hand."

"You're older than I am. I should be the one helping you."

"What's a couple of years among friends?" he said before his door shut.

She managed to get her door open. But honestly, she wasn't joking when she said that her entire body hurt.

She was moving, but it was slow enough that he had made it around the pickup and stood in the opening of her door by the time she got her seat belt off and her body twisted and pointing out the door.

"Here," he said, holding his hand out.

She put hers in it, and he froze.

He didn't move back, didn't move to help her, didn't move at all.

"Pam?" he said, low and soft. His eyes still pointing downward.

She looked at the ground. Was there a snake or something down there?

"What?" she asked, more concern in her voice than she meant for there to be.

"I just realized something."

"What's that?" she asked, truly baffled.

"You don't have a ring."

"Oh my goodness."

Her breath stopped. Her heart did too. At least it felt like it. Her mother would notice that immediately. Like, before she even had the door closed behind her. It wouldn't matter if Pam was in the kitchen or attic or bathroom. Her mother would immediately sense that there was no ring on her finger.

"It's too late to do anything about it. I told her we would be here."

She couldn't help it; her voice raised in panic. She hated to admit that she was panicking, but she definitely was. Funny how a small piece of metal could do that to her. "I'm sorry. I totally never even thought about it."

"You don't have to apologize. You did this for me."

"You did it for me."

His head lifted, and his eyes met hers, and she realized he truly was serious. He appreciated her doing it as much as she appreciated him. He really detested Stacy.

But Stacy wasn't a permanent fixture in his life the way her mom was.

"I... I have some costume jewelry upstairs, and a couple of nicer pieces too, but my mom has seen every one of them. She's the kind of person who doesn't forget an outfit or any of the accessories that go along with it."

"I suppose it would be a stretch to get her to believe that we didn't buy a ring, but you used your favorite piece of jewelry instead. But I don't like the idea of that."

"I don't either, but I'm at a loss for anything else."

"Well..." The hand that wasn't holding hers went slowly to the collar of his shirt, where he pulled down and hooked a finger around the chain that always hung around his neck.

She'd seen the ring that hung there several times. It had been his grandmother's on his father's side. She was his favorite figure from his childhood. She watched him while his mother worked and had practically raised him until he started going to school. He credited her with almost all of the good things in his life. When she'd been dying, on her deathbed, she'd given him the ring. He'd worn it around his neck ever since.

"Don't take it off," she said as his hand slipped out of hers, and he reached behind his neck.

"It will work. Actually, it's perfect. I can't believe I didn't think of it when we were getting married."

"You didn't think of it because..." Her voice trailed off. She wanted to say because it wasn't a real marriage. But if they were planning on staying married for the rest of their lives, it kind of was. Except, they were just friends, rather than romantic partners.

"No. That's not why."

"How do you know what I was going to say?" she asked, trying to sound cool but sounding curious and a little sad.

"You're going to say because it was a fake marriage. But it's not."

He didn't elaborate, and she didn't say anything more either. Wasn't it? If they were still just friends, it still was a fake marriage. Kind of. Except neither one of them were planning on ever trying to get out of it.

That made it real. Surely there were plenty of other people who were friends rather than more, who went through life together.

She kind of doubted it but realized that it was quite possible.

It didn't matter. Whether there was a precedent, whether there wasn't, she and Mark needed to do what worked for their relationship. Which was, suddenly, the most important thing.

She'd already had one marriage that didn't work out. She didn't want her fake marriage to not work out either.

But it didn't feel like there was a huge chance of that happening as Mark pulled the chain from around his neck and carefully allowed the ring to slide off it.

"I haven't taken that off since the day of her funeral," he said as he allowed the ring to fall into his hand.

"I don't feel like I'm worthy of this."

"I always intended for my wife to wear it. That's you."

She lifted her eyes to his, and he was staring at her, his face serious.

She forgot about the mud and the cold and even the pain of her muscles as she looked into his eyes.

She was his wife. Even yesterday when the judge had pronounced them man and wife and then told them to sign the papers and pay the receptionist on their way out, she hadn't felt as married as she did at that moment.

Mark was her...husband.

It seemed impossible to believe and a little bit surreal, but he took her hand without breaking eye contact and pulled it up.

"I don't have a ring for you," she murmured, even though that wasn't what she wanted to say. She wanted to tell him that she understood how much that ring meant to him, that she knew how much he had loved his grandmother, that she was honored that he was putting it on her finger, that she would try to live up to the example that his grandmother had set, but none of those words came out. Just the wrong words. But a smile ghosted over his lips.

"I think that's a little less important."

"Maybe it's good that I don't have some man's ring sitting around my house."

"I wouldn't want to wear your ex-husband's ring. It doesn't seem to have any concern for vows and keeping them."

"No. I'm not even sure what he did with it. It's probably in some landfill somewhere."

The thought made her sad. They'd been so happy the day they'd gone ring shopping together. She'd been so sure that he was the man that was going to stand beside her for the rest of her life. She eagerly looked forward to their life to-gether and had put that ring on his fin-ger with all of the dedication and deter-mination in her heart. Maybe it was just as well that it was in a landfill.

That felt a lot different than this, as Mark slid his grandmother's ring onto the third finger of her left hand.

"With this ring, I thee wed," he said as it slid into place, slightly tight but still a perfect fit.

She didn't know what to say to that. Maybe there wasn't anything to say.

The air between them felt like it was charged, and she couldn't remember to breathe. Not as his hand settled over hers, enclosing the ring between them, and as his eyes drilled into hers, and his head slowly lowered.

She found that whatever he was going to do, she wanted it. Wanted to be closer. Wanted to...seal the vows. Wasn't that what a kiss was supposed to do?

She tried to swallow through her tight throat but couldn't, even as Mark's head continued to lower slowly, his eyes holding hers as though he were watching her, maybe to see if it was okay, maybe to see if she suddenly changed into someone else, someone that he was normally expected to kiss, not his best friend.

She didn't get to find out if he truly was going to kiss her or maybe just tilt his head at the last moment and brush her cheek, because a car motor interrupted them, along with the crunch of gravel beneath car tires as her mom pulled in behind them.

"It's perfect for you," Mark said, squeezing her hands, before he straightened, and the spell was broken.

Did he mean that his grandmother's ring was perfect for her finger? Perfect for her?

She supposed she would never know, not unless she asked him, and she couldn't see herself doing that. That seemed too presumptuous, and she wouldn't want him to be afraid to do anything kind to her, fearing that she might take his kindness and consideration as romantic gestures. It would make things between them awkward. She didn't want to do that, didn't want to destroy the friendship that they built over the years by reading more into his gestures than what she should.

Now she realized that she'd never thought of Mark as a very romantic man, but his kindness and his consideration said romance louder than any words ever could.

It would be sad if he stopped doing those things because she overreacted.

She swallowed the thoughts and allowed him to thread his fingers through hers, tucking her arm underneath his and helping her out of the pickup.

Her muscles screamed in protest, but it was a silent scream of sorts because there was too much going on in her mind for her to really register the pain of her tired and aching body.

They took a step away from the truck, closing the door behind them and standing shoulder to shoulder as they walked toward her mother.

She'd forgotten how good it felt to have someone standing beside her. Someone to do life with.

Actually, it never felt that good with her ex. It had always been a bit of a toss-up as to whether he was going to stand with her, or whether he was going to take some random stranger's side and criticize her. It had made being with him stressful and not fun.

But with Mark, she never had to worry. He would always back her, especially with her mom.

Without a thought, she walked beside him to greet her mother.

Chapter 11

Mark held Pam's hand in his as he walked to her mother, Lynn.

Cradled it in his was more like it.

He wasn't sure what was going on with his heart back there, but it was doing odd things, while feelings that he'd never felt before swirled in his chest.

He'd almost kissed his best friend. That's what almost happened.

She didn't act like she realized what he was about to do. Or, if she did, he'd stunned her so badly she hadn't had any reaction at all.

He wasn't sure what was up with him.

He meant all the things that he'd said. He admired her, wished that he could be more like her in some ways. The way she treated her mom, the way she didn't allow the millions of dollars that were supposed to be hers influence her into giving up the beliefs that she held and said she believed. She actually lived them. He didn't know too many people like that. Several million dollars would make a lot of people lose their minds, let alone their religion. But not Pam.

He didn't think he could be as kind or patient as what she was. She had determined that her mother wanted the best for her and that eventually her mom would get around to giving her her inheritance.

What her mom had done wasn't the slightest bit legal, and it would take a lawyer five seconds to force her mother into doing what the will stipulated.

But Pam didn't want to lose the relationship with her mom. That was more important to her, even though her mom hadn't been the greatest mom, than all the money in the world.

How could he not...love someone like that. Of course he loved her. She was his friend. A good friend. His best friend.

Still, he couldn't use the fact that she was his best friend to excuse the fact that he'd almost kissed her. Had wanted to. He would have, if her mom hadn't pulled in and brought him back to reality.

The thing was, she didn't seem to be protesting. She hadn't pulled back or made some kind of joke, and hadn't acted like he was stepping way out of line. Which he kind of was.

They were supposed to be friends. She would be fine if he labeled her his best friend. He figured she probably considered him her best friend. And they'd been through a lot together. Now... They were going through marriage together. And pain.

His legs ached, and he could only imagine that Pam was just as sore, if not more sore than he was. He at least was used to working outside doing physical labor. She was not.

But she had been game all day, even if she did complain about being old. He didn't like to think about it, but she was right. But getting married, knowing that she would be beside him for the rest of his life, had made getting old seem...not so bad.

And he was excited about her inn-turned-school as well. That would be a fun project for them as they moved into their older years.

It would keep them feeling young. Keep them on their toes, keep them thinking about things and working and having something to occupy their time.

Maybe that was part of the reason he didn't want to give up his business or at least give up being outside. He didn't want to be depressed that he couldn't do what he used to do anymore.

"Well, if it isn't the newlyweds," Lynn said as she stepped around her car, her hands on her hips, her eyes narrowed as she looked at them from head to toe and back again.

Her mom didn't miss much, and Mark felt another sliver of anxiety weave through his nerve endings.

"Yeah. It's us," Pam said, and she sounded nervous and apprehensive and uncertain.

He let go of her hand and put his arm around her shoulders, drawing her to him. It wasn't a hardship, and she fit just fine. Honestly, he wasn't quite sure what happened to him, but he didn't want to stop touching her.

Having her closer was exactly what he wanted.

In fact, he didn't think this was quite close enough, but he didn't want to over-do anything either.

"Why didn't I know about this?" Lynn said, pointing a finger between the two of them. "This thing that you two ap-parently had, and that you were getting married? I didn't have a clue."

"I guess we really didn't know either," Pam said, and Mark had to work to close his mouth over a snort. Neither one of them had a clue. That was the absolute truth.

He liked that Pam was concerned about lying and didn't want to be dishonest. He felt that way too, and he appreciated the fact that he didn't have the pressure to lie no matter what. If her mom figured it out, Pam would admit what they'd done, rather than live a lie. He was sure of it. Even though they hadn't talked about it.

That much alone was enough to ease his mind. She was going to roll with it, whether they got the millions of dollars or not.

Although, for him, he maybe felt a little more pressure, because he knew how much Pam had riding on this. She'd given up her job, and the inn was all she had.

Now that she had a glimpse of possibly opening her own school, the money would really help.

In fact, the money was an imperative.

"Well, you do know that your girls are upset with you. They feel that, as your daughters, they should have known that their mom was on the verge of getting married."

Beside him, Pam stiffened. If there was one thing that meant more to her than anything in the world, it was her daughters.

Mark tried not to allow his fingers to curl into a fist. It angered him that her mom seemed to take great delight in coming between Pam and her daughters. Especially now that both of the girls were out of the house. It was almost as though her mom saw their affection as competition, and her mom wanted to win.

It was hard to believe that a mother could be like that with her daughter, but Lynn was not exactly a normal mother.

Or maybe she was. Maybe she just wasn't a good mother.

He supposed there were a lot of people who had a tendency toward selfishness over kindness and love. Mothers weren't immune from that.

It was one of the reasons why he really admired Pam. She had seen how her mother was and had determined that she would be different, even if it meant loving her mother when her mother did things that hurt her.

"I was out helping Mark today, and I didn't have a chance to talk to them."

He felt bad that he had been the reason she hadn't talked to her girls. But she probably needed a little bit of time to figure out what to say to them anyway.

"Pam and I wanted to get cleaned up before we ran to the diner, but you're probably hungry."

"I am. And I don't like to eat too late. Going to sleep with a full stomach gives me heartburn all night long."

He looked down at Pam, with his brows raised, asking her if she would be okay if they didn't shower.

"If you don't mind, I'll run in and change my clothes. I'll wait to take a shower until we get back from the diner."

"That's fine." He smiled. Then he tacked on, "Sweetheart."

Humor lit her eyes, as she saw what he did. He was glad she approved.

They shared a little bit of laughter between them without laughing at all before she ran off to change.

Leaving him with her mother.

"So tell me what's really up." Lynn didn't waste any time.

"Well, we were planting trees today, and it's hard to find good workers, so I married Pam just so she'd be around all the time whenever I need someone to help me."

Her mother snorted. "Like I'm going to believe that."

"Well, you don't seem to believe that I married her because I wanted to. Which is the truth." It really was the truth. He was more than willing to marry her. It had been a shock at first, but it seemed like something that was natural. In fact, when he had been talking about a honeymoon earlier, he actually thought that... Maybe he'd like to go on one. He wouldn't mind at all spending time with Pam. In fact, if he had to choose one person in all the world to spend time with, it would be her.

"I know that you guys were friends, maybe better friends than what I would like to see you be. She needs to get out with people her own age, women. Anyway, what happened? Did you guys just look at each other and decide that you like each other like lovers instead of friends?"

"Yeah." He didn't elaborate. That's exactly the way it happened. Only, they were married before he had looked at her and decided that...maybe he liked her for a lover rather than a friend. Or both. Definitely both.

"And when did that happen?"

Just a few minutes ago, but he could hardly say that. Before he was able to figure out if he could say anything that wouldn't give away their ruse, another car pulled in the driveway. It barely fit, but it didn't need to.

He recognized his sister's car immediately.

Paulette jumped out, almost before the motor shut off, and went running to him.

"Mark Gregory Shields." Her hands perched on her hips as she walked closer, and she gave him the look that only a sister who thought that her brother should be in the deepest, darkest amount of trouble possible could give. "What have you done?"

"Well, I planted trees today," he began. Only to have Lynn interrupt him.

"That's what he was telling me too. Some song and dance about planting trees. Like I wasn't here because they got married. I suppose that's why you're here too."

He didn't need to introduce them. They'd seen each other plenty of times. Occasionally they'd even gotten together for a cookout or something in the backyard with Pam's girls and Paulette's as well.

Although, his favorite cookouts were the ones where it was just Pam and him. Whether the girls were there or not, they made it nicer but not necessary. Just sitting beside the fire, looking at it, having the lake in the distance was more than enough enjoyment for him after a long day of work. It was the best way to spend their summer evenings.

"So you really did get married?" Paulette said, her eyes roving over him, then landing on his finger. "But you don't have a ring."

"In my line of work, a ring would be dangerous," he said easily, and that was the truth, although if Pam had given him a ring, he would wear it. He would rather lose a finger than not let the world know that he was taken. That he made promises, that he had a love that would never end.

All those things were true, with or without the ring. The ring just made it...a symbol that everyone could see.

"I guess that's true," Paulette said, then she huffed out a little breath and walked closer, her hands falling from her hips before they reached up to go around his neck. "I'm happy for you, truly. Just...surprised. I love Pam, but I always thought you guys were just friends. You...treat each other like you're girlfriends in high school or something."

"Yeah. Sometimes friends make the best...spouses." He wanted to say lovers, but that word tripped off his tongue. He couldn't quite get it out. Not just because it didn't apply to Pam and him, but maybe more because he wanted it to. That was a revelation that he wasn't sure what to do with. But it was a true one.

"Goodness. So sorry to keep you guys waiting. Oh! Paulette. I didn't know you were here." Pam came hurrying out, still limping a bit, and he wanted to ask about that. Did she have blisters on her foot from her boots? Or did she have a knee or hip that was more sore than the rest of her body?

Not that he wanted to talk about their aches and pains, but he actually kind of did. He cared about her. Wanted to know if there was something he could do to make her more comfortable.

Actually, he wouldn't mind having a wife rub his sore muscles, just as he was thinking that he could rub hers.

He shoved that thought out of his head, because it didn't apply to Pam and him at all, no matter how much they were trying to pretend for their family members.

"Congratulations, Pam. I guess you know how much I think of my brother, but I think pretty highly of you as well. I kinda think that maybe he got himself a good girl." She wrinkled her nose at him. "Even if I was trying to get him to pay attention to Stacy."

"I think Stacy cooked her goose when she took his dog to the pound." Pam said it in such a friendly, easy way that Paulette didn't take offense, the way she might have if he would have said it.

"You guys want to back out so I can get my truck? I offered to drive everyone to the diner, but the two of you have me parked in."

"I can back up and pull over on Pam's side," Paulette offered right away. "Although, we can just walk to the diner."

The idea of walking, even the three blocks it took to get to the diner, was not something he was looking forward to. He figured Pam probably wanted to do that even less than he did.

Still, she probably didn't want to admit to her aches and pains any more than him. Or complain about them. And once one admitted to them, it was a lot easier to complain.

But no one wanted to spend the evening with someone who's complaining about how terrible they had it, so he closed his mouth, and Pam never opened hers, and they started off walking toward the diner.

Pam and he were in front, and he kept his arm around her until they hit the sidewalk. Then, he slid it down until he was holding her hand.

Her mother and his sister followed too close for them to have any kind of whispered conversation, but he squeezed her hand, apologizing for the walk, for the fact that they were ambushed by their relatives, and for the fact that she wasn't in a nice warm shower right now but was instead walking down the street heading toward the diner.

Although, her stomach growled, and he laughed. "Maybe this wasn't such a bad choice after all."

She laughed along with him. "I'm starving. It's almost overshadowing everything else."

He knew exactly what everything else was. All the aching muscles and the soreness.

"Are you limping?" Her mother's voice came from behind them.

"I don't think so," Pam said. "But I might be. Do you think so?"

She sounded baffled, and her mother didn't say anything else.

"Smells like they're having their smoky kicky Italian sausage pasta again," he said as they got closer to the diner. He sniffed the air, drawing in the smell of delicious food and hearing his own stomach rumble in response.

"Are you guys okay sitting outside? Looks like there's room?" He knew that was Pam's favorite spot to sit, and he was gratified when she squeezed his hand.

"Oh, I don't know. I suppose if the bugs aren't too bad."

"It is not as windy as it is sometimes," his sister added.

"All right. You guys can go ahead and sit down. I'll let them know we're here."

Actually, he should have said that Pam and he would do it, but it was too late as her hand slipped from his, and she opened the gate to the patio area to allow her mother and his sister to walk through first.

Funny, he hated to be away from her for even the time it took to go in and tell the waitress they were outside. He had to laugh at himself. He was acting like a kid in junior high with his first crush. Not like this was Pam, who had been his best friend for the last ten years. Now all of a sudden, he didn't want to be separated from her for thirty seconds? What in the world was wrong with him?

Maybe this was what love felt like. Or infatuation anyway. He shook his head, having thought that he was immune to such a thing. He definitely needed to get over whatever it was, because he was sure to ruin their friendship and scare Pam to death if he couldn't get a handle on his feelings.

Chapter 12

Pam watched as Mark came back outside. Funny that she missed him for just the thirty seconds that he was gone.

Her mother was talking to his sister, and she allowed the conversation to go over her. They were complaining because neither one of them had known that Pam and Mark were getting married.

She did not know what to say. They were married, and that was that. In hindsight, she could see why they'd be upset. Maybe she would be, too. Although it seemed a little arrogant to expect people to plan their marriage in such a way as to keep her happy. She hoped she would be able to see that and get past any slight she might feel.

She had noticed her mother looking at her ring finger pretty hard and was thankful that Mark had given her his grandmother's ring, because if he hadn't, her mother would have known right away she was wearing a piece of jewelry that she already owned. Her mother had sharp eyes that way and a memory that didn't forget anything.

Mark noticed her looking for him, and she couldn't help but notice that his eyes had gone directly to her when he had stepped outside.

Interestingly, she could feel her cheeks heating. How could her best friend make her cheeks heat and her heart race? It was just Mark.

"Oh my goodness, you're blushing," Paulette said, and Pam's hands went to her cheeks. She really was blushing.

"Maybe it's just the fresh air," her mother suggested, but she looked at Pam with concern in her brows.

Why would her mother be concerned? Shouldn't she be happy?

But her mother never had the reactions that a normal mother might. Pam had long ago decided that she was going to love her anyway, but sometimes it was a difficult relationship and she wished she didn't have to.

But she was reminded, over and over again, that God loved her mother. God had loved her mother so much that He had actually sent His son to die for her. If God could love her that much, surely Pam could love her just a little.

Sometimes she was easy to love, but most of the time, their relationship felt like a minefield that Pam was constantly trying to make her way through, but never with a lot of success.

Mark settled down beside her in his chair, in one motion sliding it toward her and casually slipping his hand around the back of her chair.

All right, so she was kind of happy that her mom came to visit. After all, she liked this whole cuddling with Mark thing. It was...different but good. Good in a very nice and cozy and I-wish-this-would-last-forever kind of way.

They chatted about the weather, with her mother saying that they were due for a late snowstorm, since they hadn't had one in several years, and the waitress came out to take their orders.

She and Mark both ordered the special. Griff's specials were known far and wide for being the absolute very best thing on the menu. They often became permanent fixtures.

Thankfully, Griff and Chi had been teaching Rodney, the young man they'd semi-adopted, how to cook as well.

Rodney had a team of draft horses he'd gotten from a dude in North Dakota, starting a business giving carriage rides along the beach, but from what Pam understood, he was planning on going to college in the fall after taking a year off school.

"I have to tell you, not because I'm forced to, but because I want to, there are strawberry crumb bars for dessert, and you need to save room for these. They are amazing." The waitress tucked the electronic tablet she had in her hand into her apron as she took the last order from Paulette.

"I think I'll take one of those, maybe as an appetizer," Pam said.

"Pam! Isn't that...a little uncouth? Eating dessert first? What is your husband going to think?" Her mother sounded genuinely shocked that Pam would order dessert and eat it as an appetizer. Like there was something morally wrong with it, rather than just being a little unconventional.

"Her husband would think that's a good idea, and I'll take one too," Mark said to the waitress, who nodded her head and pulled her electronic device back out to add to their order.

"Strawberry crumb bars?" Paulette said thoughtfully.

"That's right. Griff's recipe. He made a couple of batches the other week, and while they were good, he made some improvements that made these ones chewy and soft and the flavor just bursts in your mouth, and that is the only way I can explain it." The waitress sounded like she was truly in love with the crumb bars, and if Mark hadn't already ordered some, she would have convinced him to do it just then.

"I'll take one," Paulette said right away.

The waitress smiled and nodded, punched it into the electronic tablet, then began to walk away.

"Wait. I suppose I better order one as well, or I'll be sitting here watching everyone else eat them and...wishing I had one too." Her mom sounded genuinely distressed to have to order a strawberry crumb bar. "Give me a salad while you're at it. Maybe it will help offset some of the cancer-causing agents I'll ingest with the crumb bars."

"You got it. What dressing?" the waitress asked, meeting Pam's eyes and smiling just a bit.

Her mom told her what dressing, and the waitress thanked her and walked away.

"I'm so glad you were there. I am starving, and I was hoping that by ordering the special our food would come out fast, but this way, we're going to be eating in another couple of minutes."

Mark grinned at her, and she made a mental note to remember to thank him, profusely, after they got out of hearing distance of his sister and her mom. She really appreciated him supporting her. Her mom had a tendency to do that, divide and conquer. She often tried to do it with her daughters. Whatever Pam said, she took the opposite side and then tried to get her grandkids on her side. It was annoying. And more successful than Pam wanted to admit. Her daughters were all too often happy to make fun of their mom, and while she was sure they didn't really mean to hurt her feelings, it was hurtful the way the three of them seemed to gang up against her.

She was glad that Mark didn't have any-thing to do with that.

"What made you decide to get married?" her mother asked. Again.

"I already told you. I looked at her one day and realized that I liked her for more than a friend."

Pam had glanced at Mark when he start-ed talking, and he looked at her as he spoke, and she felt like his words were…true. Actually, Mark didn't like to lie any more than what she did, and she'd never heard him utter something that wasn't one hundred percent true.

Funny that he was doing it now for her. Except, the way he looked into her eyes as he said it made her feel like he meant it.

"I know you said that, but it's just so hard for me to believe. You guys have been friends for so long."

"You know, I've heard of this. People who have been friends and never really thought about each other as more, until something has a tendency to throw them together, and then they realize that hey, we've been missing this all along." Thankfully Paulette interjected into the conversation and drew her mother's attention away from them.

Pam didn't think she had any words at the moment. Looking at Mark seemed to pull them all from her head. Not necessarily because her brain wasn't working, just because her feelings seemed overwhelming. She didn't want him to look at her like that, because it made her feel...like he really did love her.

She already knew he cared about her. Of course he did. She was his friend. His best friend. But when he looked at her like that, it made her feel like there could be more. Actually, it made her want more.

She barely noticed when the waitress brought their strawberry crumb bars out. Mark said a quick prayer, and Pam said a few words of her own. Questioning God. What was going on? Why was she having all these crazy feelings? Was it just because of marriage and all the things that that was supposed to entail? Had it gone to her head?

She forgot about all of that as she bit into the bar. It was divine.

"What I really need where I live is not the beach, but Griff. I need Griff." Paulette sighed as she took another bite of her strawberry crumb bar.

"Griff's wife might have something to say about that." Mark laughed.

"All right. Let me be more specific. I want Griff to cook for me. She can have him all the other times, I just want Griff in my kitchen."

They laughed, but Pam had to say, "You know, Mark isn't a bad cook. Actually, he's pretty good."

"Griff has me beat with all the strawberry recipes, but I'm pretty sure I can make bread better than he can."

"You know what. That's true. Your bread is really awesome, although your rolls are even better. I could get fat on your rolls."

"You can use a little bit of meat on your bones," Mark said, and she laughed, because that wasn't the slightest bit true. She already had a little extra meat on her bones and could stand to lose some. But it was sweet of him to say so.

"Maybe I'll have to make some soon," he said, and the way he looked at her when he said it made her heart smile. Like he was going to do it just because he realized that she liked them, and he wanted to make her happy.

If that wasn't what a real relationship was supposed to be about, she didn't know what else it could be.

Chapter 13

"Hey, guys, congratulations!" Chi said as she brought out a tray filled with strawberry crumb cake. "We heard that you two got married yesterday, and Griff actually made a cake this morning. We've been slammed all day, but I had every intention of walking it up to your house and getting it to you." She set the strawberry crumb cake on the table, then leaned in like she was telling them a secret. "I have to tell you, this stuff is amazing. Your taste buds will feel like they've died and gone to heaven. It is fabulous." She emphasized the last word.

Mark smiled at her excitement. He liked to eat as well as the next person, but sometimes he just didn't understand how excited women got over food. But Chi had made Pam happy, if her excited smile and the way she clapped her hands together like a little kid at Christmas was any indication.

He just looked at her. Caught up in the unaffected way she was real and genuine. She didn't pretend to be happy. She didn't watch how she smiled or how she turned her head to put herself off to the best advantage. He doubted she'd even spent any time in the mirror looking at those kinds of things. She just...was Pam. And what she said, she meant.

That was one of the things he loved about her. The fact that she didn't sit around thinking about how she wanted to act. She was naturally kind and considerate, and it came out in everything that she did. She didn't try to conform to society's idea of what a "cool" or suave person did.

He'd been around folks like that. Folks who weighed every word, concerned that they were going to be considered lame and that society would reject them.

But Pam wasn't concerned about society. Her concern was what God thought of her. Mark admired that. It made a big difference in how she acted and how she interacted with people.

"Look at that. Now that is the look of a man who is in love." Chi turned to him, and he startled, realizing that he had been staring at Pam, and he probably did have that look on his face. The look that he really didn't realize he might have been giving to Pam for a while. Because, as he thought about it, he'd been feeling this way for quite some time.

"That's a good thing. Good thing we're married. Good thing I can look at my wife like that." He didn't bother to deny it. There was no point.

Her shining eyes had turned to him, and Chi's observation had made her glow, and then his words on top of it had made her smile turn up even more.

It made his heart happy to see Pam looking so happy.

"Oh, you two are just too cute. Anyway, congratulations on your marriage. This is from Griff and me. Although he made the cake, it was my idea. So we both get credit, right?"

They chuckled.

Then Chi tilted her head. "You can tell me if this is none of my business, but there's also a rumor going around that you bought the inn. Is that true?"

"It sure is," Pam said, and her voice held happiness.

"What?" her mother said, and Pam's face fell immediately. Mark wanted to reach across the table and grab a hold of her mother. What a way to make a person feel terrible.

"You bought an inn? What were you thinking? You quit your job, and now you're buying an inn?"

"I'm happy for you," Chi said, smiling. "I know Lana is saying that the bed-and-breakfast is constantly booked solid, and the hotel always has no vacancies in the summer at all. An inn is an absolutely brilliant purchase."

"We were thinking about turning some of it into a school. Like a charter school."

"Oh. That's interesting. I bet that'll be popular as well. The kids have to be bused to Blueberry Beach, and I bet there will be a lot of people who will take advantage of that if the price isn't too high."

"I haven't thought about tuition at all, but Mark is helping me, and we are in the stage where we're just tossing ideas around. I have the teaching experience, and I'm looking for another teaching job."

"Then that's another thing we need to talk about," Lynn said, her voice low and ominous.

Mark appreciated Chi pretty much ignoring the tension that was at the table because of Lynn's injections.

"All right. We're working on your order, and it will be out shortly. But I wanted to make sure I brought this out and told you guys congratulations. You two are perfect together. And I'm so happy for you." There was no doubt that Chi was speaking the truth. He could see the love she had for Pam shining in her eyes.

He appreciated the fact that Strawberry Sands was populated with such sweet people, who always wanted the best for each other. It was a great place to live, and he thought again about how blessed he was to make his home in such a wonderful place.

Chi had barely walked away from the table when Pam's mother started in on her.

"You quit your job. You bought an inn. And you want to start a charter school?

What is wrong with you? Is this some kind of midlife crisis?"

"No. I don't think it's a midlife crisis. I see it more as God opening a door and me walking through. I'm a little bit nervous about it, but I know I want to do what the Lord wants me to do."

"The Lord doesn't want you to do anything stupid." Lynn didn't sound very nice. Mark had always tried to stay out from between Pam and her mother. When they were getting along, he didn't want them to remember that he had fought with either of them. Pam had said that she appreciated it. Appreciated him supporting her as much as he could without fighting with her mom.

It was one thing for a mom to forgive her daughter. It was quite another for a mom to forgive someone that she barely knew.

But it was hard sometimes. Lynn was very selfish and had never really grown up. She also was quite extremely controlling, and the way she tried to control Pam was by insulting and belittling her into doing what she wanted.

Over the years, he and Pam had talked about it, and Pam had gotten to the point where she knew she needed to still respect and honor her mother, since it was a biblical command, and she at the same time needed to let the insults and the belittling roll off her. She didn't need to take offense, and she didn't need to allow those things to bother her, since her mother's opinion of her wasn't nearly as important as what God thought.

Mark knew all of that but also knew that it was a difficult thing to put into practice. A person wanted to distance themselves, if not outright attack, someone who was being unkind.

"I agree. Whatever God wants me to do is going to be the very best thing for my life. But sometimes the way He works is a way that we just don't understand."

"God is the author of everything good," Lynn said.

"Not to interrupt, but this strawberry crumb cake is absolutely delicious."

Paulette, whom Mark had almost forgotten about, held up a piece of strawberry crumb cake that had one corner bitten off. "This is my third one. I hope you guys don't mind that I'm really helping you celebrate your wedding."

"I'm glad you like them. And it's nice that we have something to share. We weren't expecting company," Pam said, grinning. "And Chi was not exaggerating when she said about how good these are. I've never tasted anything like it. Wish I could cook like Griff."

"I think Griff is good at everything," Mark said, remembering that he heard somewhere that Griff had made money in Chicago, possibly at a law firm, although he couldn't remember the specifics. But anyone who could cook like Griff defi-nitely had a talent.

"You're changing the subject. What I need you to do is to just settle down and act like an adult. Not like a teenager who is chasing some fad or following whatev-er any celebrity says on TV."

"Mom. I'm doing what God wants me to do. He opened the door, and I walked through. And I'll just keep doing whatev-er it is that He wants."

"God doesn't work that way."

"Maybe that's what Joseph was thinking when his brothers threw him into the pit? That God doesn't work that way? But a lot of times, God does work that way. He leads us down paths that we don't understand. Like when Saul was trying to kill David. Surely David had to wonder if he was ever going to be king?"

"That's different." Her mom didn't elaborate on how it was different, but she seemed to think that since she said it that made it true.

Mark knew Pam didn't want to fight, and if her mom was going to leave it at that, Pam would too.

"Oh!" Chi said as she hurried back to the table.

Mark glanced up, surprised.

"I forgot!" She put her hands on the table, a little out of breath. "Rodney wants to give you two a ride in his carriage. I was supposed to ask you when I brought the crumb cake over, but I totally forgot. If you guys are interested, I'll text him, and you guys can just let him know what time you're going to be down there."

"Tonight?"

"You can do it anytime, but he said tonight would work. There's going to be a full moon, although it's not quite dark yet. And..." She looked at their clothing. Neither one of them had thought to grab a jacket. "When the sun goes down, it's going to be chilly, but he has blankets in the carriage. It's actually very romantic. Griff and I have done it a few times, and Rodney's a natural driver."

He looked at Pam, who glanced at him and shrugged her shoulders.

He nodded and then looked back at Chi. "All right. You can tell him, and we'll text him when we're done here and ready to walk down."

"Awesome. He'll be happy. He wanted to do something for you guys too."

Chi gave them one last smile and hurried away.

Well, that was one way to get away from his sister and her mother. They'd take a carriage ride together. He would much rather be on the beach with Pam than walking back to their house and having to deal with her mom the entire time. So far, his sister hadn't been too bad, but she'd been pretty busy eating. Once she was full, she was likely to start on them too.

Normally he didn't mind too much, but he was feeling very protective of Pam, for some odd reason. He didn't want her to have to put up with all the skepticism and unkindness.

"I don't think you guys should do that. I just read online the other day where a runaway horse and carriage killed a man." Paulette swallowed and brushed crumbs off her lap. "That's dangerous." She shivered.

"I don't think I've heard of any issues at all with Rodney and his Percherons. In fact, they've brought business into Strawberry Sands more than anything else, other than maybe the other stables." Just like he usually let Pam and her mother hash things out, Pam never got between him and his sister. He knew this was his baby to deal with.

He appreciated that. She would have his back, but she wouldn't step in front of him.

He hadn't realized how much he liked that. Liked the fact that he had her support, but she didn't try to control him. It was a quality in friends that could be sadly lacking.

"Well, I'm just telling you what I read. I would be careful about that. Probably a stroll along the beach would be a lot smarter." She looked specifically at Pam. "Doesn't that scare you?"

"No. It doesn't. I guess it's possible that even though Rodney's horses are the most gentle horses I've ever seen, they could spook at something, I suppose, and run the carriage off a cliff or something. I don't know. But this diner could collapse while we're sitting in it. That happens too."

"That's why we have building codes," Paulette said, getting her glass and taking a sip and raising her eyebrows.

"True. But despite building codes, things happen. Even if the building is built to code, it might fall down. My point is, anything could happen at any time. I'm not going to sit around and be afraid."

"Well, some things are more dangerous than others. Anything that has to do with horses notches up the danger level."

"I guess you're right."

Mark put his arm around Pam and squeezed gently. He appreciated the fact that she didn't fight with his sister, although she didn't allow her to intimidate her either. He knew that she valued family and the relationships that they had with them, and didn't want to put any wedges between them.

When his nieces were younger, they had been afraid that if Paulette was offended, she wouldn't allow her daughters to visit. They'd always walked around on eggshells with that, and he was grateful that they had made sure to keep those relationship lines open. They'd had a lot of good times with his nieces, and he had a good relationship with them now that they were adults.

"If you don't want to go, we don't have to."

"I think it would be fun. I've wanted to go ever since he's gotten them, but...with school, and then in the summer, they're always so busy..."

"Same. I've wanted to do it since he's gotten them, too. I... I'd really like to do it with you." There. Maybe he'd been saying more than he should, but it made Pam's eyes glow. And then her mother cleared her throat, and Pam's expression changed.

He couldn't quite put his finger on what happened, but it made him think that maybe she was thinking that he was only saying that for the benefit of her mom and his sister.

He wanted to tell her that he was being sincere. But maybe she didn't want that kind of relationship with him.

Maybe, she was just pretending.

But no. He had just been thinking to himself that Pam was always so real. She wouldn't be able to fake something like that. She couldn't.

Maybe she could. He didn't know. He just knew he wasn't faking it. And he knew that Pam had always been honest and real with him. And with everyone that he'd ever seen her interact with. He didn't want to think that there was another side of her. Hoped there wasn't.

Their food came, and it was delicious. It ended up being a nice meal, once Pam's mother stopped pressing Pam about what she was doing with her life, and once his sister stopped pushing them about doing dangerous things.

He supposed he wouldn't have minded having it just be Pam and him, and he realized that he'd always enjoyed being just with her.

After they were finished eating, Chi packaged their strawberry crumb cake up, what was left of it, and sent a container of the pasta home with them as well.

It made Pam glow again, and it made him pretty happy too.

"How long are you guys going to be? I want to talk to you tonight. I need to get back home tomorrow," Lynn pressed Pam as they walked out the diner door. She'd taken charge of the containers of food since he and Pam planned to head straight to the beach.

"I don't think it usually takes very long," Pam said, and he could hear the weariness in her voice. She hadn't gotten a shower yet, and she worked all day. Hard work, and while he really appreciated her help, he wanted to take care of her.

"I don't think you need to wait up. She doesn't have any plans early tomorrow, so maybe you two can talk before you need to go."

"I need to talk to you." His sister stood with her hands on her hips, giving him that look. The look that siblings gave. The one that said that he needed to toe the line.

Only, he had a wife now. And he wanted her to know that she was more important. Whether it was a fake marriage, whether it wasn't. Whether they were still just going to be friends, the title of wife gave her a position in his life that he was going to honor.

"After I take care of my wife, if you're still up, I'll talk to you. But we've had a long day, and I want her to enjoy her ride and be able to go home and take a shower, and get some rest."

As he was speaking, he felt Pam's hand slip into his. Her fingers threaded with his, and she squeezed, and he didn't need to look down to feel the connection. To feel her appreciation, and to know that giving her the honor that her position deserved was the exact right choice.

"Well, I'll be waiting." His sister lifted her brows at him, then she lifted her chin and turned.

Pam's mother turned with her, and they walked off.

Seeing them leave made him sigh in total relief.

He realized that as he was sighing, Pam was as well.

"Is that not just the biggest stress reliever right there? Having them walk away?" He grinned, looking down at her. Knowing that she would understand that he didn't hate them, didn't even dislike them, just... They were high maintenance, and spending that much time with them wasn't impossible, but it did feel good when they left.

"It would feel even better if they were in their cars and driving away," Pam said, and they laughed softly together.

"If you're too tired for this, we don't have to do it," he said, remembering how tough their day had been.

"I think I got my second wind. I had been exhausted there for a while, but the food just really revived me."

"I ate so much I think I can go take a nap."

"If you want to go home, we can." She lifted her brows, and she hadn't started to turn at all, backing up her words with her actions, unspoken and subtle, but still there. She was saying that she was totally fine if he didn't want to go.

"I appreciate that. Appreciate you supporting me with my sister, but not stepping in front of me. I... I love how real you are. It's something I admire about you. And I appreciate your loyalty and support. Two more things that I've always appreciated in you."

She grinned a little and looked down, as though embarrassed.

"But I really want to go. I... I wanted to have a honeymoon. I know that...our marriage isn't exactly normal." What was normal anyway? Nowadays, normal wasn't normal at all. "But still. You're my wife. I... That means something to me."

"It means something to me too. We have a relationship, regardless of how that looks, and I want to make sure I nurture it."

"Yeah. That." He didn't have those words, but that's what he wanted.

"All right then. Let's head down. Rodney just texted me before we got up and said that he was harnessing up the horses and would be ready when we were there."

"All right."

She held onto his hand as they turned and walked down the sidewalk, coming to the end of it and heading through the dunes to the beach where they walked up it a little, to get to the stable.

Rodney greeted them with a big smile on his face.

"It's not every day that I get to give newlyweds a ride. Although, it's become a popular thing." He grinned as he led the horses to the carriage.

They chatted about the weather and about his business as he hitched the horses up, and Mark was impressed with them. They were big and graceful. But gentle, and didn't flinch at all as the heavy harnesses clicked and clapped and dragged behind them.

They knew their job, and it looked like they were eager to get started.

He couldn't blame them. It was a perfect night. Cloudless sky, full moon coming up over the southern horizon, shining on the water, giving everything a pretty glow as the sun went down in the west. It was a beautiful night, and one he wouldn't mind spending with Pam, even if they were just friends.

Did he dare push for more? He wanted to. He thought about kissing her a million times since he almost had earlier in the evening.

But maybe it was the newness of their marriage, maybe the idea that she was his wife. Maybe he should wait, because he didn't want to make any moves that could potentially jeopardize their friendship. Now that they had pledged to spend the rest of their lives together, it would be awkward if he pushed for things that she wasn't interested in.

He didn't want to make anything harder for her. That was his main consideration.

So, even though it was the perfect romantic setting, as he helped Pam into the carriage, and Rodney settled them with blankets and made sure they were comfortable before he climbed onto the higher front seat at the head of the carriage, Mark determined that he would make sure that he kept the conversation light, his emotions and feelings in check, and made this about their friendship and not about a romance.

Chapter 14

"Did you ever think you'd be riding in a carriage pulled by such beautiful horses along the lake?"

Mark's voice broke into Pam's thoughts. She'd been admiring the moonlight on the water, how it shimmered and shone and sparkled. The sun was completely down, just a soft red glow on the western horizon, and a gentle breeze from the lake was fresh and clean and a little chilly. She was glad for the blankets, and after the difficult day they'd had, the motion of the carriage, the rhythmic clumping of the horses' hooves, and the occasional rattle of their harness all served to lull her into a happy state of relaxation.

"No. It never occurred to me. But I can see why people would do it. This is so relaxing. I... I could do this all night long."

"The horses might have an issue with that," Mark said, and she smiled at the humor in his voice.

His arm, which had been on the back of the carriage behind her, came down and rested lightly on her shoulders with his hand pressed against her arm, pulling her close.

"But I agree with you. This is...a lot better than I ever thought it could be. I didn't think I was a horse and carriage riding along the beach kind of guy, but I found out tonight that I definitely am." He paused for a moment, and then he said, "Or maybe it's the company."

She wanted to joke and say that Rodney was a great driver, and he had been very solicitous of them as they got in the carriage.

But after they'd started, he hadn't turned around to say anything to them. He was far enough away, with the breeze and the waves and the horses and harness that she doubted that he could make out any of their words, although he could probably hear that they were having a conversation.

Not that they were talking about any-thing private. It just felt private. Peace-ful. And relaxing.

Except Mark had said different things like that all evening. She couldn't figure out if he had been doing it for her moth-er and his sister, or because he was re-ally feeling that way. It scared her a lit-tle that those might be his real feelings, but more than fear, it excited her. Be-cause that's how she felt. It was just the idea that their comfortable relationship might be changing. Everything seemed to be changing.

"There've been so many changes in our lives. Mine in particular, with me quitting my job, buying the inn, my girls leav-ing, just... Life has been so curvy lately, and the one solid thing through all of it has been my friendship with you. This whole us having to act like we're married so that my mom believes that, I know it was my idea, even getting married, but... It makes me...anxious." She turned her head to look at him, although she couldn't make out his expression in the soft moonlight.

"Yeah. I guess marriage is a pretty big change. And we didn't exactly do it the way normal people do it, so it makes it even...less stable. I guess. For lack of a better word to describe it."

"Yeah. It just feels like my whole life has been shifting sands. I know God hasn't changed, but almost everything else has."

"You still have your health. You still have your mother."

"There are some things I wish would change," she said, but teasing mostly. Her mom was difficult to deal with, but lots of people's mothers were. If they didn't have a difficult mother, maybe they had a difficult dad, or a difficult sibling, or a difficult coworker friend or relative. Everyone had difficult people in their lives.

Some people chose to cut them out of their lives, calling them toxic and saying that they were better off without them, but she couldn't help but believe that God put difficult people into her life in order for her to become a better person herself. Or maybe to influence those difficult people. She wasn't sure, but the idea had been there. The easy way out would be to call her mother toxic and to talk to her only once or twice a year.

"You know, we spent a lot of time on the beach over the years together."

"Remember the year we had your nieces almost the entire summer?"

"That was a hard summer. I had more work than I knew what to do with, couldn't find any employees, and they were like what? Ten or twelve?"

"They were. My girls were close to that age as well, and we just had such an awesome summer."

"Really? You loved that summer?"

"Yeah! I mean, I had four girls in the house, every single day, but it was fun. We did so many cool things together."

"Man, I look back at that summer, and I think about how I dumped them on you. I mean, you volunteered to watch them, but my sister was...going through her divorce maybe?"

"I don't remember. That, or maybe her best friend had an operation."

"Oh yeah. I think that was it. Anyway, I couldn't not take my nieces, and she said they would be fine with no adult supervision all day, but she didn't understand how much I worked."

"Or maybe she was just figuring that Strawberry Sands is such a small town there wasn't any trouble they could get into."

"That might be it too."

She smiled at the memories. She wasn't joking. It had been one of the best summers she could remember. "I was actually disappointed the next summer when they didn't come."

"I remember doing bonfires. It seemed like every night."

"I really appreciated you coming home from working twelve or fourteen or more hours, and being willing to do something with us. The girls really appreciated that too. It was...like we were family."

"Yeah. That was probably the summer more than any other summer that I wished I had my own kids. I have to admit, sitting around the bonfire in the evening was so much fun. I would look forward to that during the day. That, and the fact that things cooled off at night."

"I remember you swimming in the lake almost every night after you made the bonfire. You'd jump in, saying that it had been almost a hundred degrees that day and you were going to treat yourself to a little air conditioning."

"Well, when you're mowing grass, there is no such thing as air conditioning. I've yet to see an enclosed cab on a lawn-mower."

"That would probably price them out of most people's price range."

"I think that there might be some land-scapers, like myself, who might want to splurge and spend a little extra for the convenience."

"I don't know. I guess I've never spent an entire day mowing grass, not in the summer heat. But at least you ride. It would be a lot harder if all you could do was push."

"I don't think I would be a landscaper if that's what it took. I am...getting soft in my old age."

She smiled but was quiet for a bit. It was hard to believe that her youth was be-hind her. That they really were looking at not their twilight years necessarily, but late afternoon. She didn't want to think that the child-rearing time of her life was over. Or that her body was getting old and hurting and breaking down. That she couldn't do the things she used to.

Maybe all those things were true, but she wanted to look ahead with hope and positive feelings. Like, maybe she couldn't do the things that she used to do, but she could do things now that she didn't used to be able to.

Like quitting her job and buying an inn. Like getting married to her best friend. Like having an empty nest and going to bed at three o'clock in the morning and getting up at one in the afternoon if she felt like it.

She wanted to look forward to the things that she could do and not bemoan the things that she couldn't.

But she wanted to enjoy her memories as well.

"You know, I still feel like a little girl inside, but I know I'm getting older. I want to look forward to the rest of my life but be able to enjoy looking back as well. Is that too much to ask?"

"I think it's quite possible. I mean, weren't we just doing that? Remembering the bonfires on the beach, the laughter we shared around them. Remembering weekdays, and the days right before school started when the beach was deserted, because the tourists had all gone home. But even when there were a ton of people on the beach, we had a good time."

"Some nights, total strangers would show up and just sit down with us."

"I know. It was kind of fun. The girls made some friends that way."

"I actually think one of my daughters went to college with one of the girls that she'd met on the beach. They were roommates."

"Exactly. Where else can you do that but in Strawberry Sands, right?"

"Yeah. And those are the great memories that I want to hold onto. But I guess I'm impatient to get the rest of my life started too."

"Impatient?"

"Well, maybe that's not the right word. I just think I'm getting older. I want to rush and make sure to do all things. You know?"

"Is that why you quit your job?"

"No. There is no underlying reason, other than the one that I told you about. Just a new administration, and all that, but yeah. I don't want to be in limbo. I don't want to wonder what's going to happen with my empty nest, or my job, or anything. I wanted it all to resolve right now."

He laughed. "But that's life, isn't it? It doesn't resolve. Or if that resolves, something else comes up. There's always something that we're dealing with, and I think God does that for a reason."

"I think sometimes we get it all at once too."

"It does seem like you have had a lot of changes at once. And I can see how you're in a big rush to get everything settled so that you have a predictable routine. But I suppose that's where patience comes in. Just being content where you're at right now, even if the place that you're at isn't a very stable spot."

"You and God are the only stable things in my life right now."

"The lake is still here." His words were low, soft, but they had a note of pleasure in them that made her think that he liked being lumped in with the Lord as being a stable part of her life.

"Yeah. And the town. It's changing, but not at a speed that I can't keep up with."

"And you can keep up with this. We can. Together. We'll just hang out together, be patient, and let God move and work."

"But we still can work ourselves." She wanted to remind him of that. Wanted to make sure that they understood that it was okay to work for things. But patience was usually the name of the game. She'd already made phone calls, now she just had to wait to meet with the people she needed to meet with. And to get started. And then to try to raise money. She had to be patient. Maybe they wouldn't be able to raise it all, she didn't know the end, couldn't see it, just had to wait for God to work things out.

"You know, we can always look around for the lessons that we're supposed to be learning at whatever stage of life we're in. I think sometimes we overlook that. We're so busy working on trying to get our lives together, trying to get things to work out the way we want them to, that we don't stop to think that maybe God is trying to teach us something right now."

"All right. What do you think God is trying to teach you right now?" she asked, turning the tables on him a bit, because he had been talking about her.

"Oh. That's a good question."

The horses' hooves made a muted clump on the sand, and it felt like they were the only ones in the world as the waves crashed rhythmically against the shore and the breeze blew over them.

It took so long to answer that she started thinking about the things she wanted to accomplish the next day and had almost forgotten that they were even in a conversation.

The sound of his voice startled her just a bit.

"I think God is trying to teach me patience, too. Maybe that's something He's been trying to teach me all along." He didn't really elaborate any more.

"Because of what we talked about? About getting older and slowing down?"

"Maybe to some extent. Yeah, I have to be patient with myself. Or maybe patient with the work I need to do. I have to spread it out a little more. I have to make sure I give myself breaks. I have to realize that I can't work eighteen-hour days every day all week long like I might've done back when I was younger. And yeah, some of that is learning to work smarter, not harder."

"I've heard that, and I think that that's something that people our age come up with, because we realize that we have to compensate for the things we can't do anymore."

"Right. I mean, that's part of God's plan. He makes it so our bodies don't work as well, so our focus becomes different. We look at other things, focusing on the things that we can do, rather than the things that we can't."

"Maybe that's something else we're supposed to be learning?"

"To shift perspective?" He nodded. "Maybe." He didn't say anything more, and she thought about how the Lord was doing that in her life currently. She'd always seen Mark as a friend. A good one, someone she could depend on. But now, in just a few short days, God had shifted her entire perspective so she was looking at him less as a friend and more as a...romantic interest? Something like that.

She wanted to figure it out. But that was where her lesson in patience was coming in. This, her relationship with Mark, had to play out, just like everything else, the inn, her financial situation, her inheritance, and even her relationship with her girls. She had to wait and learn to be happy in the waiting.

"Sometimes, I think when we're waiting, we can keep ourselves occupied." Mark spoke, almost as though he had read her thoughts.

"I was just thinking maybe God has us wait because He wants us to learn things. Or get better at things, or see if we'll use our time wisely."

"We only have a limited amount of time. We should be using it wisely. But instead, we want time to go faster so we get what we want, and then once we have that, we realize that it really wasn't what we wanted. Now we want something else."

"That seems to be human nature everywhere. We want what we don't have, until we have it, and then we want something else. We can't ever be satisfied."

"Maybe that's why marriages have such a hard time lasting. You look at someone and think they're exactly what you want. And then, once you're married, you think that they're not what you want anymore, and your eyes land on someone else, and you decide that's who you want."

"And it's become socially acceptable to get divorced, so you do it. Not a good thing, I don't think anyone thinks it's a good thing. But there's no stigma like there used to be, and so just because we're unhappy or incompatible, or maybe we've even cheated. And then, it's okay."

Chapter 15

Mark nodded slowly, his eyes looking with contemplation at the lake. "I wonder if there's a happy medium? A spot where we're content but still working toward a goal? I mean, if your life doesn't have a goal, if there isn't something to look forward to... Is it possible to be truly content in the moment, wanting nothing?"

Pam bit her lip. "I think it is. Isn't that what Jesus wants? For us to rest in him.

Resting implies patience. Or at least a lack of impatience. And we just rest content. We don't strive for things, we don't want what we don't have. We're just...peaceful and content."

"That's something to work toward. I know I'm not there yet. Although, I'm closer than I used to be in a way. I can't think of anything right now that I would rather have than a friend beside me, a good friend and a beautiful evening beside Lake Michigan, riding in a horse and carriage. Which is crazy, but so nice and relaxing. I'm content." He nodded, and she could tell from the tone of his voice that it was absolutely true. He was perfectly content with exactly what he had right at that moment.

"If I can push the inn out of my mind, and my mom, and all the things that I feel like I need to worry about, but I also know that worrying isn't going to fix any of it, I think I could be content too."

"It's hard to push that worry out, isn't it?"

"It is. But that's trust. Trust and patience, waiting for the Lord to work everything out."

And every time she lifted up her fingers allowing God to have His way, without trying to control everything, she got a little stronger, a little more patient, a little more willing to trust.

"The problem is, sometimes God doesn't work things out the way we want them to, and it actually looks like He's doing worse than what we can do ourselves."

"Like He's putting us through something hard that we wouldn't put ourselves through?"

"Exactly."

"I used to think that sometimes when I would make my girls do things they didn't want to. Like go to school. Or eat their broccoli. Or have a curfew. You know some of the theatrics that my girls went through, and how they thought that I was ruining their lives, and how they thought I hated them. But it was exactly the opposite. I love them, so I had to make them do hard things, or they wouldn't grow up to be productive adults."

"Yeah. I suppose being a parent kind of drives home all the things that God is trying to do with us."

"Being a good parent. Some parents don't care. It's just easier to let the kids do whatever they want to, and they never make them do the hard things. Or punish them, when they don't listen. I hated punishing them. That was the worst."

"You're not really the kind of person who is super commanding and loves to be in charge anyway."

"I think you just said I'm not bossy. I'm pretty sure that was a compliment." She grinned. They'd been having such deep conversations, which she loved. It made her feel close and connected and like they were sharing their innermost thoughts, which she'd always been able to do with Mark, which was maybe a little bit crazy. Since she was a teacher, and he was a landscaper. It wouldn't seem like they'd have much of anything in common. But they'd never had a problem talking to each other and discussing deep things that were important to both of them.

They even discussed things that really didn't matter.

"You remember all the long talks we had about whether or not Pluto was a planet?" she asked, thinking about things that really didn't matter.

"You know it is. You even admitted that I was right."

"Oh my goodness. No, I didn't. It's just a rock."

They laughed together. Neither one of them had ever been swayed from their position, but they both admitted that their positions didn't matter. Whether it was called a planet, or whether it was called a rock, it didn't matter. But they had gone through all the reasons why, all the history, even the emotional impact of removing Pluto from the list of planets, and the psychological drawbacks of children who had been taught that there were nine planets in the solar system finding out that there were only eight.

They had been fun discussions, and she looked back on them with fondness.

"We've had a lot of good talks over the years," he said, and she didn't think he realized that his finger seemed to absently trace up and down her arm.

She wanted to snuggle closer to him, not necessarily because she was cold, but because...being with him felt so good.

Anytime they'd had those discussions, they usually sat on opposite sides of the table, or one of them on a couch and the other on the recliner. Or they'd had tons of good discussions while they were cooking supper and over a good meal. Good food.

"We never really lacked for things to talk about."

"There have been lots of times where we've been quiet together. But it doesn't feel awkward. Sometimes you're just searching for things to say because you feel like you need to fill the silence when you're with someone. I never feel like that with you."

"I never feel like that with you either. I guess, I guess I don't even really notice the silences. But you're right, we've even had them tonight. They just feel natural."

"Yeah. They do. I feel like I can be myself when I'm with you."

She felt the same way with him. Like she didn't have to put on any kind of show, didn't have to pretend to be something she wasn't, or just spout off words in order to make whatever was between them feel right and good.

Rodney had turned the horses around at a spot that seemed well used, like it was his normal place to turn the buggy, and they were quiet for a while in that comfortable silence that they both had commented on.

"What do you think the odds are that my mom and your sister will be in bed when we get home?"

"I think the odds are zero for your mom, and about fifty-fifty for my sister, depending on how she feels and what kind of day she had."

"I think you're right on the money with that." She sighed a little, not looking forward to handling her mom. Her mom could be such a pill, and she had a hard day.

"Do you think you're going to be able to do it? If not, you can go in the back door, and I'll go in the front. Your mom's probably sitting in your living room, and I can let her know that you are exhausted and went straight to bed."

That last word cut off abruptly, and Pam got the feeling that they both thought of the same thing at the same time.

"They're going to expect us to be shar-ing a room." Mark's words were low and soft, and his hand stopped moving on her arm.

They'd just talked about how comfort-able they were with each other, but she didn't feel comfortable at that moment. She felt awkward and nervous and anxious and like she'd like to jump out of the carriage and stay on the beach all night.

"You're right. I...can't believe I didn't think of that."

"Well." He ran his free hand through his hair, taking several deep breaths, like the idea had upset him, and if he were on his feet, he would be pacing.

"I'm sorry," was all she could think of to say.

"It's not your fault. You don't need to apologize." He said those words quickly, with more force than distinctly necessary, but she appreciated the fact that he wanted to make sure that she knew nothing was her fault.

"It was my idea."

"I agreed. I agreed willingly. And I've actually been kind of enjoying the thought of being married to you. It's weird, I know, but it's true."

Suddenly, from out of nowhere, she thought about the night, and how they'd been together, and they hadn't taken a single picture. It had nothing to do with the problem they were facing, but she shifted so she could pull her phone out of her pocket.

"Do you mind if we take a selfie?"

He laughed. "Really? We just realized we have a major problem, and now you want to take a selfie? Tell me you're not posting it somewhere on social media."

"I just want to have it to remember. I mean, we didn't even take one for our wedding. And here we have been married a full twenty-four hours and hadn't even thought to take a picture."

"Of course we need selfies." He shifted, pulling his own phone out of his pocket.

They didn't turn out the best, since it was too dark to take great pictures, but at least they had something to mark the occasion, she thought as they both snapped several pictures.

"You know, all the times we spent together, I don't have too many pictures of you. Come to think of it."

He grunted. "I have four good pictures of you, and every once in a while, I get them out and look to see how you've changed over the years."

"You do? I had no idea."

"Yeah. Not something I'd tell you. It's a little bit weird, something that maybe best friends don't always do, but... Sometimes I just think about how you've grown and matured. You change physically as well, but the changes to me represent the wisdom and experience that you've gained. I... I cherish those pictures."

Somehow that made her throat tight. The idea that he actually had pictures of her that he knew about, that he looked at, that he thought about.

She wouldn't have thought that would make her heart flutter the way it had.

"But we still haven't solved the bigger problem."

"The fact that my mom is going to be waiting up for us and possibly your sister, and we aren't sharing a bedroom."

"Yeah. That problem."

"Well, we'll just have to...pretend."

"Yeah. I don't like that, but I think it's the best. I guess I take less clothes than you do, so do you want me to go to your bedroom?"

"I think it would make more sense if I went to yours." He was the one who owned the duplex, and although the sides were evenly divided, she just thought it made more sense for her to do the moving and not him.

"I guess I like that idea better, but I hated to suggest it, because it seems more considerate to say that you could stay in your room if you wanted to."

"I appreciate that consideration, but yeah. I agree with you. I'd rather go to your room. I just...like that idea better." She laughed a little. "It makes it sound like I'm hiding something in mine. I promise I'm not."

"Well, maybe I'll have to go over and check, just to make sure."

"You go ahead and do that. My room is your room."

"I don't think that's quite how that saying goes."

And there they were, laughing again. Even though they really shouldn't be. Or maybe they should be. They had something hard to face, but instead of getting all worried and concerned about it, she felt okay with Mark beside her. Better than okay, confident.

Even if she was a little nervous about what was going to happen once they got to his room. Talk about messing up a friendship. They'd certainly never done anything like that before. She had no idea how they'd handle it, but... She supposed that they would do it...very similar to the way they just handled it now. With some humor, talking it out a bit, and dealing with it, the way they always did.

Except, she was probably fooling herself if she thought that this was the same as everything else they faced. It had the potential to shift their relationship in a seismic way.

They didn't say too much for the rest of the ride, and although Pam enjoyed it, there was still something that nagged her the entire way.

But they thanked Rodney as he grinned from ear to ear, opening the little door to the carriage and pulling the steps out and helping them down.

"I'm just happy I have something that I could give you. A wedding gift."

"I appreciate it. It was the best carriage ride I've ever had," Mark said with a grin and a wink.

Pam and Rodney both laughed, knowing that he meant it was the only carriage ride he'd ever had too.

But she loved it, and she would love to go back for another one. Mark made her feel special, and it was romantic as well.

"We'll have to make this a yearly thing on our anniversary. A carriage ride to mark the day." Mark looked down at her, and she got caught with her mouth open, unsure of what to say.

She supposed she hadn't thought about their anniversaries in future years. She hadn't really thought this whole thing through at all. Which was kind of funny, because usually she thought everything through, but for the last week, she'd thought nothing through.

Then she smiled. At the idea of them having more anniversaries and having something to mark them.

She nodded. "Rodney, you count on it."

"Well, I'd definitely like to. But I'm probably going to college next year. But I have an idea of someone to take my place. So the horses will be here, and the carriage, hopefully, and maybe once I'm done with school, I'll be back."

"I hate to see you leave Strawberry Sands, but I understand." Mark held his hand out, and Rodney looked surprised, then he grasped it and shook it, and Pam smiled as it seemed like his chest puffed out even more.

She appreciated Mark doing that, making the kid feel so good. But he was used to working with kids that age. He hired a lot of high school and college kids who were on break over the summer to help in his business.

It had helped him know how to relate to her girls, even though he usually worked with boys. It showed character to be teachable, to learn how to deal with people, to know that he was the boss, but instead of leading from a position of power and authority, leading by relating to people and working with them. Pulling rank when he had to, of course, because there was never any doubt that he was the boss, but making sure that each of his employees knew that they were valued and wanted.

She'd often wished she worked for such a great boss.

They bid farewell to Rodney, and as they turned to walk up the sand to the side-walk, Mark took her hand again.

It felt natural this time, and she thread-ed her fingers with his easily. Loving the way it felt, loving what it said, and wondering if maybe they were moving toward a shift in their relationship, but a good one. One that...felt natural, the way the rest of their relationship would surely feel.

She hoped so.

Chapter 16

Rodney watched Mark and Pam walk away, feeling good deep down in his chest the whole way to his toes. He loved the fact that he'd been able to give them a little gift for their wedding. It wasn't very often that couples got married in Strawberry Sands, although there had been a rash of weddings in the last few years. If one or two weddings per year could be considered a rash.

Still, it gave him hope. Hope that he'd be able to go to college and come back to Strawberry Sands and be able to make a living. He loved it here. His parents had always looked at it with derision, because it was poor and rural and not as classy as Blueberry Beach, but it had the same wonderful people, who looked out for each other. He wanted to be a part of that. Offering a ride as a wedding gift was just one way that he was able to give back a little to the community.

He couldn't believe how good it felt.

He hummed softly to himself as he walked around the carriage to the heads of his horses.

He'd fallen in love with them the day that Cord Stryker had brought them, and he took care of them like they were his children.

He named them Cinderella and Ashley and called them Cinders and Ashes for short.

"Hey there, girl," he said as he walked around the near side of Cinders. She wore blinders, but she moved her head and nuzzled his ear.

Both of them were over eighteen hands high, and they towered over top of him, even though he was an easy six foot, but he loved the feeling of power that he had when they both pulled the carriage. He loved walking with them too.

"Hey there, Dixie. You're out late."

He smiled, recognizing Becky's voice right away.

"Bekpet," he said, using the nickname that he'd called her since the first few times he'd seen her struggling to get into his bedroom, trying to find food.

It was funny, the tables had totally changed on each of them. Becky had been adopted by a really great family, who'd even adopted her sister. She was happy in her home with Kristin and Luke, even if her adjustment time had been a little rough.

He on the other hand, had come from money and privilege, but his mom had shot his dad and then shot herself. There had been money left for him, eventually, although it had taken a while to get everything straightened out.

Now it sat in an account, and even though he'd offered to give it to Chi and Griff for taking him in and allowing him to live with them, they refused it.

It was his, whenever he wanted to use it. He just… He was happy with his Percherons, his carriage business, and while he wasn't excited about the idea of going to college, he thought it was going to make Griff and Chi happy if he did, so he had plans to do so in the fall.

"I can't believe you're allowed out this late. Your parents know where you are?" he asked, trying to be the big brother he was supposed to be to her.

She was growing up, looking less and less like a belligerent little kid and more and more like a beautiful young lady. She was still just in her mid-teens and way too young for him, but... There had always been something about her that had drawn him.

"They know where I am. I told them I wanted to come talk to you, and they said it was fine. Dad saw you driving along the beach and said that you'd be unhitching your carriage and rubbing your horses down and I could give you a hand if I wanted to. So I came."

"I see. Are you going to just stand around and talk, or are you actually going to help me?" he said, giving her a hard time.

"You need to lead the horses so they park the carriage first. I've done this a few times, you know," she said, lifting her brows and giving him a superior look.

It was true, he always had the horses pull the carriage to where he parked it in a lean-to along the barn. He covered it as well, trying to keep it nice.

He had a hold of Cinders's lead as he clucked to her, and both horses started out at a slow walk. Although, with legs as long as theirs were, their slow walk ate up ground quickly.

Becky was almost jogging trying to stay ahead of the big hooves. Neither one of them would hurt a fly, but if they stepped on her, it was going to hurt,

even if their feet were as big as dinner plates which definitely spread the
weight around. Still, a ton was a ton, and
it hurt when that ton was on top of a
foot.

"So, you didn't get enough work in today,
or what?" he asked as he made a big
loop with the horses and they circled
around, heading straight for the barn
and lean-to.

"I dunno, I guess I just haven't seen your
ugly mug in a while and figured I'd come
make sure you didn't have the pox or
something."

"The pox? Isn't that like a sixteenth cen-
tury thing?"

"I don't know. I just want to check you out to make sure you aren't going to die anytime soon."

"Why? You think you're going to inherit something?"

"I don't want anything."

Her voice sounded a little depressed, and it made him look at her.

"Anything?"

"Nothing money can buy anyway. You know, there's more important things than money in the world."

"Oh. Wow, that's wise coming from a twelve-year-old."

"I'm fifteen."

He grinned. He figured if he gave her an age that was younger than what she was, she'd get all offended, and he could hear in her voice that she was annoyed. He couldn't help teasing her. He liked to get her riled up. She was so cute. Although, there was something else about it, something that drove him to want to tease her when he didn't typically have that problem with anyone else.

Although there was something serious he wanted to talk to her about.

"I forgot you're getting so old. Where's your walker?"

"Shut up, Dixie. Why did I come out here to help you anyway?"

He stopped the horses, and Becky was already walking toward the back of them to unhook the traces and the carriage tongue.

He tied them at the hook he had for that purpose before he followed her back.

"You know, I'm heading to college in the fall."

"I know. I heard."

Of course she did. It was a small town. She knew everything about him probably.

"Then you heard that I was hoping you would take over my carriage business while I was gone."

Her head jerked up at that. He knew she hadn't heard. He hadn't talked to anyone about it. Not even Griff or Chi, although they probably suspected.

"Really?" There was excitement she couldn't contain in her eyes, and then they lowered. "But I could never afford horses like this."

"Oh, I wasn't going to sell it to you. I just wanted you to take care of everything while I was gone."

"What do you mean? Feed your horses?"

"Do the bookings, buy the feed, muck out their stalls, make sure they have pasture, and when they don't, feed them hay. Take care of their hooves, polish the carriage, and all the things I do."

"But… But how?" Then she shook her head. "Of course I'll do it. Do you really trust me?"

He looked down into her upturned face. Despite the fact that she was fifteen and growing up almost before his eyes, there was something childish and insecure about the look that she gave him. Like she was that homeless little girl, who was just searching for a family to love her and would do anything she could to hold onto the one person she had in the world, her sister. The little girl who was hungry and didn't have anyone who cared whether she ate or not.

She'd grown by leaps and bounds since Luke and Kristin had adopted her, and he knew they loved her beyond words. He heard Griff and Chi talking about it, and he'd seen with his own eyes the sacrifices they made for the girls they had.

But he supposed that maybe Becky was like him. There would always be some scars from the things that she'd gone through.

He wanted to protect her, wanted to ease that hurt, wanted to reassure her that there was at least one person who would always love her.

But he didn't want to tell her that he loved her. She might take it wrong. Or maybe that was taking it right, and she'd know he was romantically interested in her. But she was too young, and he was too old, and he was leaving in the fall anyway.

"Of course I trust you. Who else would I get to do it? I can't think of anyone in the world I would trust more than I trust you. How long have you been taking care of Davis's horses and you haven't killed even one."

He had to add that last line on, just to put some humor in the situation and keep it from getting too serious. He didn't want her to know that he struggled with the feelings that he did.

Becky and he were destined to be always friends, never more. And he wanted to make sure that things didn't end up being awkward. After all, Becky would be a good and loyal friend for the rest of his life.

"That's true. It's been three years, I think. More. And yeah, I'm taking care of them all, and he always says I do a good job."

"Plus, Cinders and Ashes love you. And they're familiar with you."

"Did you decide whether you're going to breed them or not?"

They finished unhooking the carriage, and he flipped the long traces over the back ofAshes on the near side before he went up to untie them and lead them into the barn where he would remove the harness.

Becky waited for him, following along behind in case the traces came off.

Once they had the gentle giants tied up in the barn, they worked together unhooking them, beginning with the ties that held them together before they took each individual harness. As they worked, he answered her question.

"I was thinking about doing it this winter. Or maybe late fall. So they have their babies after the tourist season is over, and the foals will be ready to wean before the worst of the tourist season starts in the spring."

"That would be good timing."

"Yeah. I even have a stallion in mind. Cord has a big gray stud that is just drop-dead gorgeous, is a little taller than my girls, and he sires really great foals. Cord said since we bought Cinders and Ashes from him as well as the carriage, he'd give us a discount on the stud fee."

"But?"

"Well, I'm working around my schedule, but it might not be the best schedule for my girls. You know, having a foal in late fall isn't ideal. And they might not even come into heat."

"Is it dependent on the light or something?"

"A little, I think. I need to read up on it more. Breeding is a pretty big deal, but Cord said he and his wife would even come in for foaling if I wanted him to."

"It's so nice to have someone who is willing to give their time and expertise to help you get started."

"That's part of the reason that I chose to go to college in North Dakota. I'll be closer to him. Just a few hours away. He... He said I could come out to his ranch on holidays and weekends if I'd like. He said he'd put me to work."

Rodney laughed a little. Cord and his wife had been so kind and helpful to him. They nurtured his love of horses and encouraged him in his efforts to learn more.

His parents had never been supportive, and he kind of shoved the idea of horses aside when he had been growing up.

It was nice to have people who saw that he had potential and encouraged him to nurture that.

He tried to do that with Becky. Not just because he liked her, not just because it was the right thing to do, but to pass on what other people had given to him. Also because he liked her. He truly wanted to see her succeed.

She loved horses too. It was something they had in common. Now more than ever. Although he had gotten her her first job at the stable.

"Are you serious about wanting me to take care of your horses while you're in college?"

"I sure am. You're already doing it for Davis. There's whole weeks that he doesn't go down to the stable because you have everything in hand."

"He calls me his stable manager, and I just give him a weekly report. I suppose he goes down when I'm not around, but it's true that he lets me handle everything. Even the bookings now."

"I'll have you do that for me too. I'm working on getting the website set up along with some QR codes so that people can book online, and you won't get very many calls."

"I couldn't do it while I was in school. Although, they let me out two hours early so that I can go to my job. They call it a work-study thing, and I actually get credit for it. Everyone else has to stay in study hall." She grinned.

"That sounds just like you to get out of school as much as you can. Although, I bet they have to chase you out of the cafeteria."

"Stop it. I don't do that anymore."

She laughed, but he thought she was a little sensitive to that. Which was kind of funny to him in a way, because she was so skinny. It wasn't because she didn't eat, although that's the reason that she'd been skinny when he met her.

"All right. We'll have to spend some more time together at some point while I show you everything. But I'll keep things as simple as I can, and the hard part is working with the horses which you already know how to do."

He hefted the last harness up and carried it over to the peg in the wall where he hung it when it wasn't in use.

Becky already grabbed a currycomb and was brushing out Cinders.

They hadn't worked up a sweat. It was cool out, and he hadn't worked them hard at all. The girls could trot all day and not even breathe hard. They were true workhorses, and there was just something about working with them that gave him such a good and complete feeling inside. He couldn't imagine spending his life without them.

As he watched, Becky pulled over the step stool that she needed in order to reach to the very top of Cinders's head.

She was a good bit shorter than he was, almost a foot, and she still had to reach up on her tippy-toes to get to the top. But that didn't stop her. She was the kind of girl that nothing would stop. She was gritty and determined and tenacious. He admired all of those things. He'd been developing those things in himself. Maybe it was because of his easy child-hood, but he didn't really have much in the way of any of those things when he had met Becky.

Anyone who looked at them would say he was the one who helped her, but in reality, she taught him a lot about life and about character in general. He owed a lot of the direction that he was going now to her.

They worked in silence for a while, with Becky leaving after they walked the horses out to the pasture and let them loose.

He watched her walk up the sidewalk, humming to herself as she did. He noted she did not turn around and look behind her.

He wasn't quite sure why she'd shown up, but he suspected that she worried about him. He appreciated that, that someone cared enough to worry, but there was a part of him that even though he knew it was for the best for her not to, he wished that she cared about him, the way he cared about her.

Chapter 17

Mark tried not to grip Pam's hand too tightly as they walked up the steps to their duplex.

His side was dark, but there were lights on Pam's side, and he could see the silhouettes of two heads in the living room.

Great. Both of them had waited.

He wasn't exactly afraid of Pam's mom, but she could be intimidating and also very...difficult. Pushy. Everything that

Pam wasn't. It was kind of funny how opposite she was from her mother.

Living with someone like Lynn had made Pam the person that she was. He'd seen over and over again how the hardships in someone's life had turned them into a better person.

He knew the Lord did that for a reason, but knowing that there was a reason didn't make dealing with the difficulty any easier.

"Ready for this?"

"Yeah. Can't be any harder than dinner was."

"The food was good anyway," he said as he opened the door and grinned at her.

She returned that grin, and just a glimpse into her eyes, where she said more than words about how much she enjoyed being with him, bolstered his spirits.

"You took a long time. Surely there was no one in line at this time of night?" Lynn said, looking up from the knitting she held in her hands.

"Especially this time of year," his sister added, glancing up from her phone.

"There was no line. We just had an enjoy-able ride. It's a beautiful night out. Did you guys see the full moon?" He spoke, giving Pam a little bit of time to orient herself.

"It's cold outside. I want to stay warm, not see the moon. It's been up there every day that I've been alive. Nothing new about tonight." Lynn was dismissive.

"It's pretty. And romantic." Pam glanced around at him, and her cheeks pinkened.

Maybe it was because she was saying the moon was romantic while she had been with him. Maybe she was feeling that there was something more between them as well.

Instead of talking about her mother, he should have talked about the direction of their relationship. Maybe that was a discussion they should have at some point. Although, it was a tricky discussion, because the reason that he hadn't had it was because he didn't want to ruin what they had.

He shelved that idea.

Although, communication in a relationship was supposed to be key. Surely if he put his foot in his mouth, their friendship was strong enough to withstand it.

He'd have to think about it.

"All right. Well, we're going to go to bed. We just wanted to come in on this side and make sure that you guys were okay? Paulette, you can use any room, including the one you usually stay in, if you want to. Mom, you can use either of the bedrooms upstairs. I don't have mine cleaned out yet, but both my girls' rooms have clean sheets and towels."

"Okay. I just wanted to sit with Lynn, so I didn't miss you guys coming home. I wasn't sure whether...you guys had moved in together or not."

"Maybe they've been living together all this time."

"We haven't. Pam just told you that her stuff is still in her room. We've only been married for a day, and we worked all day today. We haven't had time to move anything."

He wasn't going to allow Pam's mother to start any rumors like that. Although everyone in Strawberry Sands saw them go in their own doors. Although, they also saw them go in each other's doors too. They probably spent just as much time together as they did apart. If one didn't count sleeping, it was more.

"I'll stay in my regular room, if it's clean," Paulette said, looking at him.

He kind of wanted to have her stay on Pam's side, to give them a side to themselves, but he couldn't lie.

"Both rooms are clean; you can sleep in either one."

"All right. I guess I'll go ahead and stay in my usual one. I assume you guys will be over soon?"

He nodded, looking down at Pam, who looked exhausted.

He put an arm around her. "It's been a long day. We are heading to bed, but we wanted to make sure that Lynn is going to be okay here by herself."

"I'll be just fine. I might be old, but I'm not incapable." She spoke matter-of-factly and made no move to put her knitting aside.

Paulette said good night and walked out the door.

"We'll probably have breakfast in Mark's kitchen tomorrow, although I haven't talked about his workload for tomorrow, so we'll see how that is. I have a meeting at eleven at the inn, so breakfast will probably be around nine or nine thirty. If you come over, we'll cook for you."

"I don't know if I'll be up that early. I like to stay up later at night and get up later in the morning." Lynn's knitting needles clapped together. "But I will be over at least to say goodbye to you. I'm heading home, and you probably won't see me after your meeting."

"All right. Good to know. Maybe we can invite you and the girls over for supper soon."

"You'll have to do that."

"Night, Mom," Pam said, and it twisted Mark's heart to hear the note of sadness in her voice. He wished that she had a better relationship with her mother, but he didn't know how to make that happen.

It made him sad.

With his arm around her, they walked to the door, he opened it, and they stepped out. He was tempted to stay outside. There was so much rolling around in his mind, so many changes, and so many things he wished he could fix and couldn't. Then there was the matter of them going to the bedroom together. That could be awkward with Paulette upstairs as well.

But he didn't stay out; he opened the door to his side of the duplex and allowed Pam to walk through first.

Whatever happened, they'd get through it together. They always had. That was one thing about Pam and him, they were so comfortable together that things just kind of naturally worked out. He was hoping that this was going to be the same as everything else.

They went to the kitchen, got a drink, and washed their hands, then, still without saying anything, they walked up the stairs.

She knew where his room was. There were different times over the years where he'd been sick in bed, not too many, but about five years ago, he'd had the flu really bad.

She brought him chicken broth and eventually rice soup, and she helped him go to the doctor.

Other than that, she hadn't been upstairs in his house much, but at least she knew where he slept.

Indeed, she went straight to his room, with him following. From the light coming underneath the bathroom door, he assumed that was where Paulette was.

They walked in, and he closed the door behind her, turning on the light.

"I don't have any clothes," Pam said right away, turning around to face him, concern puckering her brow.

"Mine will be too big, but I have plenty. They'll work for tonight, won't they?"

"Yeah. I guess I should've thought about it. I mean, I told them that I didn't have time to move my room, so it wouldn't have been strange if I would've gone up to get clothes. I just...didn't want to. Didn't want to bring that kind of questioning into anything. After all, I should have something over here."

"Not necessarily," he said, grinning and hoping that his joke wasn't too off-color for her.

She looked at him in confusion for a moment before she chuckled a little. "Okay. I suppose that's right, but it's a little awkward."

"It's not that awkward. Just don't think about it like that."

"It's hard to think about that any way other than naked," she muttered, crossing her arms over her chest and walking to his dresser. "Where are your T-shirts?"

"Second drawer down. Underwear's first drawer, although if you borrow my underwear, I might need you to actually show me that."

"All right. No underwear." She opened the second drawer and rummaged through, pulling out his blue Yellowstone State Park T-shirt that she always said was her favorite. He teased her it was because of the bear on the front, but she always insisted it was because of the color.

Regardless, he smiled when he saw that she went to it immediately. "What if that one hadn't been clean?"

"I'd root through your dirty clothes until I found it, of course. This is the only T-shirt you have worth wearing."

"I have a green one you like."

"Oh. That's right. It's the one you brought back from Ireland."

"Yeah. I have two nice T-shirts, and now you're stealing one and we've only been married a day. This is ridiculous."

She laughed, as he hoped she would, and the anxiety and tension that had been in the air dissipated.

"Pants are four drawers down. I have some sweatpants in there that will drag on you, but they'll work."

"Awesome. Although, I might have to use underwear. I'm not sure I can stomach the idea of not."

"Well, just remember, you swim in my underwear, I get to see it."

"Seriously. You do not want to see me in your underwear. It's going to look ridiculous."

"I know. Why do you think I want to see it?"

"Because you thought I would be sexy?" she said, tossing the words over her shoulder as she dug in his drawer for the one pair of sweatpants that were slightly short on him. It was funny that she knew which ones they were, black with a stripe down the side, and his favorite pair actually, because they were kind of like the old wind pants that were hard to find anymore. For some reason, they were extremely comfortable.

"You know what, I'm just taking a pair of underwear. You don't get to see it, so stop asking."

"Well, I'm not sure what you're going to do for that other type of underwear that you need."

She turned, holding a pair of his underwear in her hand, with his T-shirt and sweats hung over her other arm. She looked confused for a minute before understanding dawned that he was talking about a bra.

"I was assuming you didn't have any of those," she said slowly. Then she bit her lip. "Actually. I'm hoping. Really hoping. That you don't have any of those."

He grinned. "Maybe you should have questioned me a little further before you agreed to marry me."

"I really hope you're teasing me," she said, closing her eyes and acting like she was truly wishing.

He laughed. "I just heard the bathroom door open. You can have it first. I know you're really looking forward to that shower."

"I was. I still am. Are you sure, because I know that you worked just as hard as I did, more so."

"I planted more trees, but that doesn't necessarily mean I worked harder. And I'm sure. You go on."

He had to change the bedsheets. He couldn't remember the last time he'd washed them, and if Pam was seriously going to sleep in his bed, he wanted her to at least have clean sheets.

He didn't mention that though. He really didn't want to admit that it had been so long since he'd washed the sheets.

It wouldn't surprise her. She probably already knew it, but... There were just some things a guy wanted to do and wanted to have a semblance of privacy while he did them.

Chapter 18

Pam hung her towel up and took one last look in the mirror. She looked like a drowned rat, but Mark had seen her look far worse. Actually, it was an improvement over the frizzy hair and dirty face that she'd been sporting all evening and not even realized it.

Still, she adjusted the too big T-shirt and pulled up the too long sweatpants. She tried to open the door with one hand while holding both legs of the sweat-pants up with the other.

There was something...intimate about wearing Mark's clothes. She'd seen him wear these things a hundred times. She picked the T-shirt out because it was her favorite. It was worn into a soft, almost silky feel, and although she thought it looked far better on him than it did on her, she loved it.

The sweats were his favorite, but they were also the smallest ones he had. They fit her better than anything else.

She had to admit, she understood why they were his favorite. They were ex-tremely comfortable.

Thankfully, she did not see Paulette as she walked down the hall and turned to go in Mark's room.

The door was closed, and she almost knocked, but that would have been weird, especially if Paulette had happened to step out in the hall at that point in time.

Mark stood with his back to her, his shirt off, but still wearing pants, thankfully.

He dug through his T-shirt drawer and pulled a shirt out as she stepped in.

He turned around with his second favorite green shirt in his hand.

"All done?" he said, probably needlessly, which was a little bit weird, since they didn't usually have a whole lot of extra unnecessary words between them.

She nodded. Not really trusting her voice to speak.

He grinned. "You look far better in that T-shirt than I do."

She laughed. "And I was thinking the opposite. You fill it out much better than me." She hurried on, not wanting any more comments about who filled out what. It was a little bit...too close to things that friends didn't say to each other. "I left my dirty clothes in the bathroom. I... I'll get them tomorrow."

"Sure. Or I'll wash them. Whatever." He shrugged, walking over with his clothes in his hands. "I'll take a quick shower, and then I'll be right back. I know you're probably tired and want to get to bed."

"Yeah. If you don't mind, I'll probably get in and read on my phone until you get back."

"That's perfect."

For some reason, her feet wouldn't move, and he'd ended up stopping in front of her. Her mouth was dry, and she had trouble sucking in air. Where had all the oxygen gone?

"Pam?"

The way he said her name sent a shiver down her spine.

"Yeah?"

"Are you okay? We can do something different if this is bothering you. People that are married don't always share rooms."

"No. We want this to be believable." She tried to lick her lips, but it was impossible as dry as her mouth was.

"True. But making it believable is secondary to me to making you comfortable."

"I appreciate that. You're always thinking about me, and I can't ask for more." She tried to smile, but it was wobbly.

"What's up?" The clothes dropped to the floor as his hand came up to touch her cheek.

"I don't know. I... I just...don't want to ruin anything that we have. You know?"

Something crossed over his face. Some emotion she couldn't name, but he nodded. Even as his hand trailed down her cheek.

"I've been thinking the same thing. I... I can't say that I mind anything that we've been doing, but I cherish our friendship too much to allow this marriage thing to get in the way of that. But I was also thinking that our relationship has been so solid that I think it can withstand this. As long as we're careful."

"I think you might be right. I hope you are. I just feel so comfortable with you. Except now. I feel a little...vulnerable. It's not an uncomfortableness as much as it's a..."

"Fear?" He lifted his brows, searching her face as though trying to find the answer there.

She laughed at how silly she was being. "I'm old."

"I'm older."

"I'm not twenty anymore. I don't look like a twenty-year-old, I don't feel like a twenty-year-old, I don't think like a twenty-year-old."

"And I'm thankful for that."

"I just..."

How was she supposed to explain to him that maybe she wanted to move forward in whatever direction they were going in their relationship, but she'd been out of any kind of relationship for so long she didn't know what was expected any-more? What a person did.

How a person was brave enough to be so vulnerable when they no longer had the perfection of youth. Far from it. She sagged in all kinds of places that a woman wasn't supposed to sag in, and she had wrinkles and bulges, and she looked like she was a mother of two girls, a woman who could be a grandmother any day. She didn't feel like that, not her heart.

She felt young still, but when she looked in the mirror, it was obvious in the lines around her eyes and around her mouth, the age spots that dotted her face, and hands and arms, they were even on her legs, although he couldn't see them now.

It made her feel like maybe she would be hurt if they tried to move forward and he was disappointed in her. Like he could really hurt her, even without meaning to.

She would have thought she was too old for that.

"You just what?" he prompted after what felt like a long time.

"I'm old, and I look old. Under these clothes is an old lady's body. It's humbling. I guess."

"I'm just as old as you are." He grinned a little. "Maybe there's a little bit more pressure on me, because not only do I have an old man's body, but things don't work quite like they used to."

He winked at her, then he said, "We're not gonna worry about that. Not tonight. You're tired, so am I." She shifted as he reached for the door, then he paused. "I don't know if this will ease your mind at all, because I'm not sure exactly where you're going. But the way you look doesn't matter to me at all. It hasn't for the last ten years. I mean, I love your smile. I'm not gonna deny that. But more because it makes me happy to look at you smiling. Makes my heart feel good to think that I make you smile sometimes."

"You make me laugh a lot."

"But I guess maybe at my age, I'm less concerned about the way you look than the way you act. The character that you have. The way you're kind to your mom even though sometimes I want to throttle her and don't understand how you can continue to be patient with her. The way you're kind to my sister. The way you take care of me. Even when I make things difficult for you and get a little grumpy when you try to mother me."

"I don't try to mother you."

"You do. But that was the wrong answer. You're supposed to say 'you don't get grumpy.'"

"All right. That's true too. I don't mother you, you don't get grumpy, and... You're silly."

"I try. Be back in ten."

She shook her head, realizing that her mouth was no longer dry, and she no longer had that pressing weight of anxiety sitting on top of her. He made her laugh, made her feel better, and eased her mind, all without really knowing what the problem was.

"Those are words I never thought I'd hear you say." She wrinkled her nose at him, and then turned with lifted brows, and walked to the bed without turning back around.

"Still sashaying around like a twenty-year-old," he said, laughter in his tone as he slipped through the door and closed it behind him, not giving her a chance to respond.

That was okay. The only response she had was to turn around and stick her tongue out at him, but the door was already closed and he didn't see it. Which was probably just as well, because a woman of her advanced years shouldn't be resorting to such childish displays of emotion, but she didn't have any other words.

She probably should thank him for making this so easy. Thank him for making her laugh. Thank him for making it feel like it was a natural thing. Shooing her off to bed like it was something he did every night.

She smiled, pulling the covers back and smelling the freshness of clean laundry detergent.

He'd changed them. The thought made her smile. Unless he just washed his sheets, which she knew he hadn't done it that day, since they'd been planting trees all day.

The idea that he'd taken the time to make it clean for her made her feel warm and cozy.

He had all of his things on one night-stand, so she chose the other side, setting her phone down, realizing she didn't have her charger, and getting in bed and turning off the light.

She didn't settle down on the exact edge of the bed, but she settled right in the middle of her side.

Might as well. He was going to act like everything was normal, she might as well too.

She wasn't going to hug the edge and act like she was scared to death of him. Because she wasn't.

She must have been more tired than she thought she was, because she never heard him come back in the room.

It wasn't until the bed tilted down on his side that she opened her eyes and realized she'd fallen asleep.

"Mark?"

"Sorry. I heard your breathing and figured you were asleep. I was trying to be quiet."

"No. It's okay. I can't believe I fell asleep. I hardly ever do that."

"Sleep?"

"No. Fall asleep while reading." She felt around for her phone, realized it was on her chest, and grabbed it, reaching over and setting it on the nightstand.

She settled back down where she was as Mark adjusted himself on the other side.

"I never even thought about your charger. If you hand your phone to me, I can plug it in."

"No. It'll be okay until morning. You're leaving, and I'll have time to charge mine tomorrow."

"All right." He was quiet for a minute, and then he said, "So we can put something down the middle of the bed if you want to? I thought about doing that myself, but when I decided you were asleep, I wanted to do as little as possible to wake you up."

"I'm okay. I know you're not going to do anything."

"I was talking about protecting myself actually."

"You're so ridiculous."

"This has to be your new favorite word. I think you've used it several times tonight, and all in conjunction with me. I don't get it. I'm a serious, respectable, elderly person, you know."

"You're not elderly."

"I'm older than you."

"You remind me of that all the time."

"Because you forget. When you call your-self old, you're calling me older."

"All right. I'll try to remember."

"Anyway, I haven't slept with anyone…in decades. A long time ago, I was told I tossed around a lot. Just wanted to apol-ogize in advance if that's what happens."

"All right. Same. Although, I don't think I snore, and I don't think I will move a lot, but in case I do. Sorry."

"Now that we have that settled, you still good?"

"Yeah. Thanks."

"Good night."

"Good night," she said. Wanting to tell him that she appreciated everything he had done for her over the past two days.

But not wanting to start a new conversation about that. He was tired, and he needed his rest.

It seemed like she barely closed her eyes when she opened them, and it was light out.

She was warm and comfortable and felt like she had the best sleep that she had in years, if not decades.

She didn't want to wake up, cocooned in feeling more safe than she felt in she couldn't tell how long.

Her eyes popped open when she realized that it was because sometime during the night she'd snuggled up to Mark, and he'd wrapped his arms around her, spooning with her from behind.

She smiled. She should be horrified and should struggle to get over to her side, but... She liked the way it felt.

"You're awake," he said, his voice a little rough and gravelly next to her ear.

"Yeah. Have you been awake long?"

"For an hour or so."

"For an hour?"

"I didn't want to get up. Sorry. This just feels...good."

His words made her smile. "I agree. You've really been awake for an hour? What about work?"

"I'm the boss. If I don't show up for work today, no one's gonna care except for me. And I feel like this would be an enjoyable, if not profitable, way to spend my day."

"All right," she said, knowing that they weren't going to spend the entire day in bed, but wanting to enjoy this just a little bit longer. Tonight, her mom would be gone, and possibly his sister too, and she'd probably be back over in her own bed. The thought made her sad. She wouldn't wake up tomorrow morning with Mark's arms around her, his legs twisted with hers, and his solid heartbeat against her back.

So, even though she knew she probably shouldn't, she closed her eyes and enjoyed the feel of the solid, honorable man behind her.

She didn't know how long, didn't have a watch, couldn't see a clock, and her phone was over on the nightstand. Way too far for her to reach over. Plus, doing that would break the spell that seemed to settle around them, and that would mean it was time to get up.

"I've been thinking about tonight."

Like he could read her mind.

"Yeah?"

"I enjoyed last night. If you ever decide to move in for real, I just want to let you know that would be fine with me."

It made her happy but also made a slice of panic tear through her. Could this be a permanent thing? She liked it, but change was always hard. And this was a huge change. A change of monstrous proportions.

"All right. Maybe we can think about that? For now, I better get up. I'm going to run downstairs and go over to my room." She wasn't running away. Not really. "Hopefully, my mom won't be up, and I can change my clothes over there with no one the wiser." Probably she should have gotten up earlier, hopefully Paulette slept in this morning as well. She wasn't known for being a morning person.

She didn't want to, but her anxiety drove her to slide out of his arms, grab her phone, and make sure she was covered in all the proper places with his T-shirt pulled down and his sweats pulled up before she stood up and hurried to the door without looking at him.

She didn't need to look at him to feel his eyes on her, with her bed head and her droopy T-shirt and baggy sweats. She probably looked like a bag lady. Or homeless.

She had her hand on the knob and was just about to turn it when he said, "Pam?"

He said her name the same way he'd said it last night, the way that made shivers run down her backbone and something warm twirl around her heart.

She stopped but didn't turn around. It was embarrassing to stand here like that. Even if she were twenty years younger, her best look was not the moment she got out of bed in the morning.

"I just wanted you to know that you're beautiful."

Her toes curled, and her fingers tightened on the doorknob.

His words made her throat tight and her heart feel like it was soaring free from her chest.

She smiled, but it also made her tear up because she knew it wasn't true.

"I can hear you thinking you don't believe me. And I'm just telling you, when I look at you, I see beauty. Inside and out."

She didn't know what to say, didn't know how to thank him for that, how to tell him that he had to stop saying things like that because she was already so close to falling in love with him. And that would ruin everything. Their good friendship, the camaraderie they shared, the easy companionship that lay between them. Didn't he know that she was on the verge of throwing it all away? Just because he made her feel like so much more than just a friend.

She turned the knob quickly and hurried out of the room, knowing she should say something but knowing she couldn't.

He shouldn't have said that.

Mark lay in bed for a few moments after Pam hurried out of the room, his hands tucked under his head, his legs crossed, but his whole body wishing that he could just cringe into a ball and disappear. What was he thinking? They were friends. Sure, they got married, and yeah, they'd slept in the same bed last night, but it wasn't supposed to mean anything. They just needed to have the relationship be believable for her mother and his sister.

And yet, it was believable, not because they were pretending, but because what he felt was real.

Staying in bed and castigating himself about it wasn't going to solve anything, and he knew it, so he got up and got dressed, wondering if there was something he could do to fix things.

He just couldn't keep the words from coming out of his mouth though. Because she was. Beautiful. Maybe not the kind of physical beauty that would draw a bunch of attention in a bar or something, but because of her giving heart, the compassion she showed, the love that she had for her students, and the way she gave her entire self to help them be better. The way she was such a great friend. He could depend on her. She would cook him supper just as easily as she put her boots and jeans on and went out into the woods to plant trees with him. Whatever he needed, she was beside him.

And she didn't demand that he do the same for her, although he tried to. She just took whatever he gave and called it enough.

How could he not think she was the most beautiful woman he'd ever seen?

Still, he was frustrated with himself that he couldn't have given her more time before he allowed the words to come out. Maybe, if they were close enough, in this forced proximity that was their marriage, she might come to feel the same way he did.

But he'd managed to ruin it.

He made his bed and then made his way downstairs. He would cook breakfast, since she didn't say, but she was probably sore from yesterday. He was. Although, that hadn't even been on his radar to think about.

He'd been so busy thinking about Pam and how he could be the same to her that she was to him.

He smiled, thinking about waking up with her in his arms. She hadn't acted shocked or upset. Maybe that was a start.

"Hey, sleepyhead," his sister said as he walked into the kitchen.

"Good morning. You're up early."

"Well, I just got a call from my girls—"

The door opened as she said that, and Ginger and Kay, his nieces, tumbled into the hall.

They were in their twenties, with careers and lives of their own, but he loved that they still considered his house home enough that they didn't feel like they needed to knock.

The door closed behind them with a loud bang, and then they squealed as they saw him down the hall in the kitchen.

"Uncle Mark!" they called as they ran to him.

He caught one in each arm and squeezed them tight. He had so many good memories with his nieces. He was so grateful to his sister for allowing him to have time with them. Of course, she used him as a babysitter, but he didn't mind at all. It was an honor to get to spend time with the two of them and to have a hand in helping to raise them.

"What are you guys up to?" he asked, after hugging them and letting them go.

"What are we up to?" Ginger said, giving her sister a raised brow and then glancing over at Paulette. "The question is, what in the world are you doing?"

"How could you get married without telling us?" Kay said, crossing her arms over her chest and tapping her foot on the floor.

"It happened kind of suddenly. That's all."

Where was Pam? Usually she made her way over to his kitchen, or else he headed over to hers. He didn't like doing this by himself. Not that he couldn't handle it, he just...felt more complete when he had Pam beside him.

As though him wishing for her had conjured her up, she opened up the back door to the kitchen and stepped in.

He knew there was a huge amount of relief on his face, but he couldn't help it.

Just in time, he remembered that they were supposed to be married, and he didn't have to try to keep himself from walking over and putting his arm around her and saying, "Good morning, beautiful." He dropped a kiss on her forehead, although he wouldn't have minded giving her a different kind of kiss. And he thought that would have been okay, even a good thing to do in front of the girls.

To his surprise, he felt her arms come around him, and she gave him a squeeze, lifting her head and smiling up into his face.

"Good morning," she said, and he found himself unusually speechless, staring down into her eyes.

He'd heard about time being suspended before, and getting lost in someone's eyes, and other romantic things that he couldn't think of off the top of his head, and he'd always considered it all rather ridiculous.

Which was kind of funny, since it was happening to him at that very moment.

His breath caught, and suddenly his hands felt sweaty.

"Guys. Hello? We're still here?" Kay's voice cut through his brain fog, and it felt like his feet touched back down in reality.

Too bad, because he was enjoying whatever was going on between Pam and him.

She looked a little flustered too, as her cheeks turned pink and she ducked her head.

He liked that. Maybe there was more going on with her than what he thought.

"If you want me to cook breakfast, just say so. You don't have to do any of this beating around the bush, hey, I'm still here, kind of thing," he said, turning but slipping his arm further around Pam and holding her to his side.

Not to show them what a great couple they were, but because he wanted her there.

He didn't want to let go. Didn't want to stop touching her.

Call him crazy, call him a fool for punishment, but it was the truth.

"Of course we want you to cook breakfast. Why do you think we're here?"

"To make sure I'm really married?" he said, making it sound like that was the obvious reason.

He gave Pam one more grin, squeezing her waist, and then he let go, walking over to his refrigerator to pull out his sausage and eggs.

"And for the breakfast, Uncle Mark," Ginger said, rolling her eyes as she walked over and put her arms around Pam, her sister at her side.

They hugged Pam just like they had him, and it made him smile to see it.

Pam was just as much a part of their lives as he was. Since she'd been there for everything that he'd done with them for the last ten years.

Pretty much all his nieces' memories and activities with him had included Pam and her girls.

"So we're eating breakfast over here?" Pam's mother's voice rang from behind her as the back door to the kitchen opened.

"We sure are. Come on in and sit down. Guess I need to get the bacon out too." He went back to the refrigerator.

"Hey! Are you here?" He recognized the voice that came down the hall as belonging to one of Pam's girls, but they sounded so similar that he wasn't entirely sure which one. He looked and saw Marilyn, with Hilda right beside her, coming in where his nieces had just entered a few minutes ago.

"I might need to borrow some food," he said in a stage whisper to Pam.

She laughed and rolled her eyes. "I didn't realize we were serving breakfast to the entire family this morning."

They chuckled together. It never bothered him when the whole family got together and he was the only man. He thought about it a few times, and he and Pam had talked about it a few times. How funny it was that their family was mostly a family of women. It didn't really affect him now, except the dynamic had changed a bit now that he and Pam were...together. Except, he was having trouble remembering if it was for real or for not real.

He really needed to talk to Pam.

"I'll run over and grab what I have. I know I have at least one package of bacon, and I think I have a pound of sausage in the freezer."

"Awesome," he said. "And I can get it. You don't have to."

"Let me greet my girls first."

Her words were shy as she looked at him with her brows lifted.

He nodded. "You go on." He knew that it bothered her more than she let on that her girls spent more time with her mother than they did with her. She felt like her mother probably tried to get them to like her better like it was a competition. Pam didn't typically complain about it, but it would bother anyone, he was sure. Even Pam, who sometimes seemed more like a saint than a regular human when it came to the patience she had with her mother.

He took a moment to watch as Pam took several hesitant steps forward as her daughters came down the hall. Not as quickly as his nieces had, but they didn't seem upset. Not like Lynn had suggested they might be earlier.

Indeed, as they reached their mother, both of them put their arms out to hug her.

"Mom! You got married again!" Marilyn said.

Mark stopped at the door, watching. He didn't want to miss this, not if Pam needed him for backup.

"You said you would never get married again. What's up, Mom?" Hilda stood back, with an arm's length between her and her mother, and tilted her head. "Although, I always knew you and Mark were perfect for each other. I told you that like a hundred times growing up."

"You never said that," Pam said, laughing.

"I didn't? Well, I thought it a hundred times. I just figured that you'd be upset if I said that, because you guys were such good friends. You never seemed to see how gorgeous he was."

"I'm gorgeous?" Mark said, laughing.

"You used to be, before you got old," Marilyn shot over at him. And everyone in the kitchen laughed. Pam's girls had always been able to tease him just as easily as his own family.

"Well, someone's not getting breakfast this morning," he said, eyeing Marilyn.

"Like you would ever not feed me. You cook better than anyone else in the state of Michigan, except possibly Griff," Marilyn said with a truly affectionate smile. "And I'm going to give you a hug too, but first of all, I have to give my mother a hard time. It's not every day in one's life that one's mother gets married, and she did it without me." She put her hands on her hips. "And you did it without me too. And you've been like a dad to us all our lives."

"It was a quick thing. We just...decided it was time. I mean, when you've been friends for more than a decade, and you suddenly realize that you've been missing out..."

"And you too, Mom. Mark has always been such a catch."

"I know," Pam said, turning her eyes on him and making him feel warm the whole way from the top of his head to the tips of his toes. There she was, holding his gaze again, and freezing him, making it impossible to move or to look away. How did she do that?

"Mother. What gives? Why didn't you invite us to the wedding?"

"There really wasn't much of a wedding," Pam began.

Mark hated to leave, but he had to go get the extra food. Or people were going to be hungry.

They were deep in conversation and laughter by the time he got back, and were standing at the stove with three skillets going, one for sausage, one for bacon, and another one for eggs.

He had grabbed a loaf of bread from her apartment, since they'd used the last of his for sandwiches the day before, and he also had a package of frozen sausage and one of bacon.

He and Pam worked together while their families chatted in the kitchen, with them joining in.

It felt good and cozy, and even Lynn behaved herself.

He couldn't believe that they'd never considered combining their families before. Never considered getting married. But the thought hadn't even crossed his mind. He had been the blindest man on the planet.

He put a hand on Pam's back as he waited for the next pieces of toast to pop up.

She lifted her head and looked at him. "It's kind of crazy in here this morning," she said low, underneath the chatter of the rest of the ladies in the kitchen.

"I kinda like it. It's our families, blended. Why haven't we done this before?"

She knew what he was talking about. There had been lots of times where everyone had been together, although Lynn and Paulette weren't always around. But oftentimes when he had his nieces, her girls were there, and the girls were almost like sisters.

They fought like sisters, but they also loved each other and got along like sisters as well.

"I don't know. After all, how could I not notice that you're gorgeous." She said that with a little bit of ironic humor in her voice.

"I think we already had this discussion. I told you last night I'm an old man."

"And I told you last night I didn't care."

Her face was sincere, and he believed her completely. Not that he didn't the first time, but it was obvious from the way she spoke that she meant every word. She didn't care. She felt the same way about him that he did about her. It wasn't about his appearance or about his age, whether he was old or not. It was about him. Whatever she saw in him that she felt was worth admiring. Or possibly loving. Could he be that blessed?

"All right, you two. Tell us your story. When did you guys figure out that you were perfect for each other?"

"When did you decide to get married? And why didn't you tell us?" Ginger added.

"Well," Pam said as she grabbed the spatula and stirred the sausage in the skillet. "I think we were just talking one evening, and we never really thought about ourselves as anything other than friends."

"I know I sure didn't. But marriage just seemed like a logical step."

"Come on. What about stars and romance and slow dancing and—"

"Lots of kisses!" Hilda said with a laugh.

"I think Mark and I have always had a solid friendship. And that's what we've built this on. It's more than just kissing and all of the romantic things you see in movies. It's..."

"Trust and admiration and the fact that I know that she has character. That she keeps her word."

"That he's not going to cheat on me or leave me."

She said that with such conviction that he had to put his hand on her waist again. Just to give her that reassuring touch. She'd been cheated on; she'd been treated badly by her first husband. The fact that she would go into a marriage with him, not afraid of those things, trusting him, made him feel like she'd given him a gift that was priceless.

"What? I know I can. Trust you that is."

"And she has the kind of character that I've always admired. She's compassionate and kind. She's determined to do her very best, wherever she is. And she sticks with her convictions."

"I wish you wouldn't stick so hard. She threw away a perfectly good job, with excellent retirement benefits, just because she had some kind of crazy convictions," Lynn muttered from the table where she sat.

Thankfully, Pam's daughters didn't seem to agree with her.

"I don't know. The more I thought about that, the more I admired you, Mom. I mean, I would be scared to death to quit my job with no prospects." Marilyn looked across the table at her grandma and then across the kitchen at her mom. "I mean, I've spent a lot of time thinking about it. You... You bought an inn, but you have no income. Aren't you scared?"

"Maybe that's why she got married," Hilda said, setting forks around the table next to the plates she already put down.

"That's pretty smart. He's got a great job; maybe that's why they got married."

"Guys. We're right here," Mark reminded them.

"I know. But it does seem kind of odd that she quit her job, and then all of a sudden, you guys get married."

"Actually, I think we were talking a lot about me quitting my job, and that's kind of where the one thing led to another, and we realized that we wanted to get married." Pam lifted her shoulders, then turned back to the stove, flipping the bacon.

Mark studied the eggs in the skillet. It irritated him that they thought that Pam might be using him. He wanted to defend her, but he couldn't say that he stood to benefit just as much as Pam did. Maybe not monetarily, but who knew what Stacy was going to do when she came this time, considering how much havoc she caused the last time.

"I don't suppose that you're going to be able to host Stacy this summer?" Paulette spoke up, almost as though she were reading his mind. "Maybe she could stay on Pam's side of the duplex?"

"I think we're going to be too busy. Plus, if you guys come, we won't have enough places for everyone to stay." Pam spoke immediately. And he appreciated it. He didn't want to tell his sister her friend couldn't stay, but he definitely didn't want Stacy coming. There was the havoc that she brought in his business, but he didn't want anything she did to touch Pam either. And if Paulette was truly trying to get Stacy and him together, he didn't want Stacy to come between Pam and him.

"I think there's plenty of room at the bed-and-breakfast. If she books now, she could probably book for the entire summer."

"She can't afford it. That's the problem." Paulette's mouth pulled back, but she didn't say anything more.

"Mark and I haven't talked about it at all, but we can discuss it." Pam looked at him, and he nodded. They could talk about it later. Both of them would want to help someone who seriously didn't have a place to stay and would be out in the cold without a helping hand. But he also didn't want to have someone there who was just going to cause trouble.

It wasn't long until breakfast was done and the dishes were cleaned up. He remembered that Pam had a meeting with the renovators at eleven o'clock.

He wanted to get her alone so he could talk to her a little bit before she left. They barely had any time to actually just talk that morning, and he wanted to be sure they were still on the same page.

They were all sitting at the table, and Mark was ready to ask Pam if she'd like to take a short walk with him, when there was a knock at the door.

Pam got up before he could stand. "I can get it," she said.

He got up behind her. It could be someone for her, but it was most likely someone for him since they'd knocked on his door.

But when Pam got to the door and opened it, he saw it was Lana Landry, from the bed-and-breakfast down the street.

She held a casserole dish in her hands.

"Hello!" Pam said as she opened the door wider so Lana could come in.

Mark got there in time to take the casserole dish from her.

"That's for you, and you, since we have heard that you two finally got married," she said, emphasizing the "finally."

"We sure did. Come on in. We just finished breakfast, but I'm sure we can scrape together a few things to feed you."

Lana followed him down the hall. "Oh, I already ate. And Sunday is cleaning the rooms in the bed-and-breakfast, but I wanted to be sure to give this to you before I took a walk on the beach."

"This is awfully nice of you," Pam said as she peeked under the aluminum foil after setting the casserole on the counter. "Oh my goodness, it smells amazing."

"Thanks. I put together a little casserole, just a little something to save a little bit of work for you guys since you're newlyweds." She greeted all the people in the kitchen, knowing them all since they'd all spent time in Strawberry Sands.

It was a thing for small towns to deliver casseroles, and Mark was a little bit surprised they hadn't gotten more.

"I just heard last night. Congratulations," Lana said, looking like she was seriously happy for them.

"The rumors are true. And I couldn't be happier about it," Mark said, taking another step and putting his arm around Pam. He seemed to take every opportunity he had to do that, and it wasn't to solidify the fact that they were in a relationship, it was because he enjoyed standing with his arm around her.

"Well, you guys are just the cutest. And I've always thought that you made an excellent couple. But you have such a solid friendship, I hated to say anything because sometimes when you get a little bit of romance in a friendship, it can make the entire thing blow up. Even though the friendship is really strong."

"We thought about that, but we decided we would just go ahead and do it," Pam said, smiling up at him. He grinned back down, thinking about how accurate her words were, even though they probably didn't say exactly what Lana was expecting them to say.

By the time Lana left, it was time for Pam to hurry off to her meeting at the inn.

Mark stayed behind, entertaining their family and cleaning up the kitchen.

While he was doing that, he had a couple of ideas, and he decided that he would head to the inn and try to have a little bit of time to talk to Pam after her meeting was over.

Chapter 20

Lana walked to the beach, the wind blowing her hair, holding a small casserole for Joe.

Joe seemed to be declining, and the last few times she'd visited him, she'd been worried about him.

It wasn't anything she could put her finger on, he just wasn't as...robust as he normally was.

Plus, she thought he was losing weight. That was hopefully something she could do something about. Even if she couldn't talk him into going to the doctor as she had been trying to do.

The lighthouse came into view before she saw Joe out in his usual spot on the beach.

She did a double take when she saw that there was someone sitting beside him.

Joe never had company. Even the son that he talked about, and who gave him the chocolate-covered espresso beans that Lana was addicted to, had never been there when she had visited. Although obviously he visited at least enough to restock the chocolate-covered espresso beans supply.

Regardless, Lana found herself hurrying a little faster as she thought that maybe she was finally going to meet this young man that Joe often talked about but who Lana had never met.

She smiled when she saw that Joe had made sure that there was a third seat beside him.

She often sat down while he fished, and that third seat said that he didn't want her to feel left out if she showed up while his son was there. She wondered if he had done that every time he had visited. The thought made her a little sad because he would have been disappointed each and every time, since she'd never come when his son was there.

Of course, maybe he brought his own seat out. That was a possibility as well.

By that time, she was within fifty yards of the men, and Joe looked up and saw her.

"That's the girl I've been telling you about. The one who eats all the chocolate-covered espresso beans."

What a way to be introduced, Lana thought as she finished walking the distance toward them.

First of all, she wasn't a girl, and second, it was a little embarrassing to be pointed out as the person who ate all the espresso beans. That was a lot of espresso beans.

But it was done now, and she couldn't erase it. After all, she was female, and she did eat the espresso beans.

The man, the son, turned his head, and she saw him jerk a little, as though he were surprised. Then, he stood to his feet, unwinding his legs like a jungle cat standing up from a nap.

She couldn't help but admire him. Even if he was older than what she had thought he would be. She figured that Joe was younger than what he appeared, since he worked on the water, outside, and the elements often aged a person faster than folks who worked inside for a living.

But as she reached for the man's out-stretched hand, hearing him introduce himself as Pierce Pianse, she realized that Joe must truly be as old as he seemed, since Pierce had to be about her age.

"Nice to meet you, Pierce. Finally." She smiled, carefully balancing the casserole with one hand while she shook his with her other.

"Let me take that," he said. "I assume it's for Dad?"

"Yes." Her eyes went to the man sitting in the chair. She didn't want to talk about how worried she was about him in front of him.

As though Pierce had read her mind, he said, "How about we walk to the lighthouse together. We'll put it inside."

"Hey. You're stealing my company. Maybe she came to talk to me. Did you ever think about that, son?"

"And she'll talk to you for as long as she wants to, Dad. She's just gonna walk me in the house first."

Lana got the feeling that she was in some kind of trouble. It was an odd feeling, and one she hadn't had in a long time. How did this man make her feel like a little girl again? When she was his age or possibly older.

Still, she didn't turn down the invitation, because she wanted to tell him what she had observed about his dad.

They turned together and started walking up the beach, toward the sand dunes and the lighthouse.

"You visit my dad quite often, according to what he says."

"And according to what he says, you never visit. But I knew that had to be wrong, since there always seems to be a fresh supply of espresso beans waiting for me whenever I show up."

"I brought those for my dad for about a year, thinking he was really enjoying them, when I realized that he wasn't eating them but was giving them to some stranger."

"I'm sorry," she said, unsure what else to say.

"It's not a problem. I just thought it was funny. Here I thought my dad was really enjoying them. But what he was really enjoying was sharing them with you. How could I not continue to bring them, when it gave him such happiness to give them away?"

Interesting. She liked the way he looked at it. From what Joe had said, she had gotten the feeling that his son didn't visit nearly enough, and that he was somewhat occupied with his business in Chicago, neglecting his father at times.

But the story Pierce had just told made it seem like he wasn't neglecting his dad at all.

Interesting how there were always two sides to every story. And a person's actions could be construed in different ways.

"I'm glad you're not upset about it. I really do enjoy them. But I'd give them up if it were something that bothered you."

"Doesn't bother me. I'm happy to bring them. It gives me a reason to come. I think Dad's been lonely. I appreciate you visiting him as well."

"I do think he's lonely. And I enjoy visiting him. It gives me a reason to get out of the bed-and-breakfast, and the walk up the beach always leaves me feeling invigorated. Plus, he's a fun fella to talk to."

"He has some good stories, I'll give him that." The man took another step before he said, "I understand you recently sold the bed-and-breakfast?"

Lana nodded, thinking that nothing had really changed. She sold it, and she had the money in her bank account, although Matt had helped her invest some of it. But her daughter and her husband who had bought it from her wanted to build their own house and had done so, allowing her to continue to live where she always had. Now though, instead of being responsible for all of the bills and financial aspects of the bed-and-break-fast, she got paid a fair wage and had a lot more free time and a lot less stress and hassle. She couldn't be happier with the way things turned out. She only hoped that her son-in-law and daughter felt the same way.

"I did."

"Now you have more freedom?"

"I do. I still work there, but no stress and headache." They reached the lighthouse, and he opened the door, allowing her to go first.

Interesting. She walked through, trying to keep from smiling. He was from Chicago. She had been sure that he had lost the manners that he'd been surely raised with in rural Michigan.

"I understand you're in business in Chicago?" she asked, truly curious. Joe had talked about his son, but never too much about what he actually did for a living.

"I do. I own several of them. I acquire businesses, consolidate them, sell them, make deals and things like that. Sometimes deals worth hundreds of millions of dollars, and sometimes they're much smaller. It's fun, but it does take a lot of time. I appreciate having someone here to keep an eye on Dad."

"He's proud of you."

"I'm all the family he has left. I'd hate for him to not be proud of me."

"He loves spending time with you too."

"I hope you're not trying to guilt me into spending more time here?" he said as he put the casserole on the counter. "Can this go in the refrigerator?"

"It can. It's cool. I carried it the whole way from Strawberry Sands."

"You really walk the whole way up the beach?"

"It's only a few miles. Not far." And they were good for her. She needed to get out and move around more. She had a tendency to stay at home and fiddle around the bed-and-breakfast. Getting out, getting in the fresh air, stretching her legs, and getting some exercise was really good for her.

"I wasn't trying to guilt you into anything. Although, your dad loves to see you. That's a fact."

"I know it." He sounded a little sad, like he wished he could be there more.

"I wanted to mention that I was bringing the casserole, mostly because I wanted to, and I often bring him something to eat, but he's looked a little more frail to me over the last few weeks or so."

"I have a doctor's appointment set up for him for next week. I've noticed that too."

"Good. I'm glad you're on it."

"That's part of the reason I wanted to make sure I talk to you."

"Oh?"

"Yeah. I was hoping that you could help me keep an eye on him."

"Of course. You don't have to ask. I'm doing that anyway. And I enjoy it. I consider Joe a friend."

"He's blessed to have friends like you."

She noticed the wording and wondered at it. "You're not moving back?"

"I can't. I'm needed in Chicago."

"Your dad needs you too." She didn't mean to give him a hard time, and she wasn't sure why she was pushing him.

She didn't usually butt into people's lives and try to tell them what to do.

"I suppose you're right. But business calls."

"You feel like you're doing good in the world?" she asked, unable to understand what would keep someone from helping their parents when they needed it.

"I'm making money."

That's what she thought. It was always money that was more important than family or people. Folks got so mixed up. And by the time Pierce figured out what was really important, his dad would be gone.

"Is your dad the only family you have?" Joe had never mentioned if Pierce was married, and she got the feeling that he was either single or divorced with no children.

"I had a wife at one point. We had a child together, but she divorced me, got a big settlement out of it, and I haven't heard from her in over a decade. Maybe two. I've lost count."

"Do you see your child?" Why in the world was she being so nosy?

"No."

"You should think about fostering children."

He didn't say anything but just stared at her. "So you've known me for exactly five minutes, now you're telling me I should foster children? Maybe I've spent time in jail for molesting one and I'm not fit to foster."

"Your dad never mentioned that."

"Because it hasn't happened, but you didn't know. You'd just shove kids off on anyone."

"I know your dad. Plus, you seem like a responsible person. And I get that your business is important. I'm assuming that you have plenty of downtime where you have recreational activities that you enjoy."

He inclined his head, as though agreeing.

"But none of that stuff will matter eventually. I bet you have a big empty house, a child that doesn't live at home anymore, and there are a lot of children who could use a good home. You look like you'd be a good dad."

She shook her head at herself, unable to believe that she was being so...pushy.

"I'm sorry. I'm not sure why I said all that, but... I guess I just know that there are a lot of kids who could use some help. I've been considering it myself."

"Fostering children?"

She nodded. "I just sold my bed-and-breakfast, and I have plenty of money to live on. If I'm careful. My son showed me how to invest some of it, and I'm hoping that eventually I'll be able to live on just the interest. In the mean-time, yeah. There are so many kids who need a family, how can I just relax and enjoy my retirement when I could be doing something to change a life? Isn't that kinda selfish of me?"

He stared at her, finally shifting from one foot to the other while he crossed his arms over his chest. "I like it better when we talk about what you should be doing and not me."

She got the feeling that those were honest words, pulled from his heart. She appreciated the fact that he wasn't trying to hide anything.

"But my life would have to change drastically in order for me to have time for children."

"Well, this might be a good time for change," she said, her chin lifted.

She'd probably never talk to Pierce again. So, it most likely didn't matter that she was challenging him almost.

But just in case, she said, "And if you have any advice for me, I'll certainly listen to it. I... I don't usually push myself on people the way I've been pushing on you. I'm not sure why."

"I guess everything happens for a reason," he said, and he didn't seem upset.

"I'll keep an eye on your dad."

"Let me give you my phone number. You can call me or text me if you notice anything. I... I'm not expecting you to check him every day, just as often as you normally do. If that's okay?"

"It is," she said, pulling her phone out of her pocket.

There was something about Pierce that made her feel...odd. That was the only way she could explain it. He made her remember that she was female. Not in an overly powerful way, just in a way that made her act out of character apparently.

Regardless, she typed in his number as he gave it to her, then sent him a quick text so he would have hers.

"Do you mind keeping me updated in case anything happens?"

"I don't. I think Dad would want me to. I'll let you know how the doctor's appointment turns out next week."

"Thank you."

"Thanks for coming in with me. I didn't want Dad to overhear that."

"No. I didn't want him to hear me telling you that I was concerned about him either. He... He is not going to get old gracefully, I assume."

"No. It's going to be a rough road. He's so used to being independent. But... You made me think anyway."

"All right. I suppose you've done the same for me. And by the way, thank you for the chocolate-covered espresso beans. I do truly enjoy them."

He smiled, and she felt like most of the tension between them dissipated. Even though if she could do it over again, she wouldn't have mentioned anything about fostering children or criticized him for his recreational activities when he could be using his time to be a blessing to people in the world. She didn't usually push her ideals on other people, and this was an anomaly that she hoped she did not repeat.

They walked out together and sat down, talking to Joe for several hours.

She enjoyed speaking with both of them, Pierce was well read and had an understated sense of humor that she enjoyed.

He was definitely a mature man, and by the time she left, she wished she could somehow find a way to ask his age.

Maybe she could get it out of Joe the next time she visited, although if she asked him outright, she was sure that Pierce would hear about it, and she didn't want him to think that she was interested. Even if she was.

"All right. I'll see your crew next Tuesday." Pam stood at the door while the folks from the renovation company filed out.

There had been three of them, and they had been excited about this job.

The entire time, Pam wondered if her mom was actually going to give her her inheritance. Maybe she shouldn't have jumped the gun like she had. After all, she had the money in her savings account to begin payments, but she didn't have enough to continue, and she wouldn't have anything to live on if she had to use it all for this.

She needed to talk to her mother.

She hadn't had a chance that morning, because the kitchen had been full. Although, she was using the full kitchen as an excuse. She'd been too...engrossed in Mark to think about anything so banal as talking to her mom about the millions of dollars that were a part of her inheritance.

Maybe it was just her imagination, but he seemed more handsome than ever this morning. Which made her feel her age even more.

He hadn't shaved the night before, and the stubble on his face gave him a slightly rugged look, even if some of it was coming out gray. She actually liked that look better. It made him look distinguished, which is what gray hair did to a man. For a woman, it just made them old.

Which was how Pam felt when she was next to Mark. Old. Even though, as he kept pointing out, he was older.

But he didn't seem to care. It didn't seem to bother him at all.

She wasn't entirely sure whether he kept putting his arm around her, dropping kisses on her head, and giving her that look that made her toes curl, saying her name in a way that made every hair on her head sigh, just to put on a show. If he was, he was a better actor than she ever thought he was.

As though her thoughts conjured him up, his truck came up over the hill.

She smiled. Her mother could wait.

The car with the renovation folks in it had disappeared, and she stepped out the door of the inn, onto the porch. The foundation was solid, but they were sending their crew in just to be sure. As long as that held, the renovations that she wanted shouldn't take more than two months, they had said.

She couldn't believe she could be an inn owner and possibly a charter school superintendent in less than two months.

She had a lot of red tape to wade through in the meantime, but the meeting today had left her hopeful. Very, very hopeful.

"It must've gone really well," Mark said as soon as he got out of his truck, slamming the door behind him and carrying the binder that he used on jobs.

Her eyes caught on it, and her brows furrowed. What was he doing with that here? Did he want her to go over some things? Sometimes he'd ask her what colors went well together or would look good in a certain area.

He was the one with all the knowledge of what plants grew where, but when it came to design, he often got her insight and input.

"Yes!" she said, unable to contain her happy smile. "I couldn't have imagined it going better. I guess the only thing that would've made it nicer would have been if I would have been able to talk to my mom before the meeting and been sure that all the plans I was making are going to be paid for."

"Well, I know that our house has been full, but I talked your mom into staying, because she was going to leave right after breakfast. So, she's going to be here for another night. That should give you an opportunity."

"Really?" she said, so happy that he had realized that she would want to talk to her, and not over the phone. Sometimes her mom could be pretty short on the phone, and it was hard to figure out how to take her.

"Really. Don't think I was going to for-get?"

It reminded her again of how much he paid attention to her. Sure, he wasn't perfect. He did forget things, so did she. But more important than whether or not he ever forgot anything was the fact that he put the effort into remembering.

"I really appreciate that," she said, stopping in front of him, smiling up at him.

"Really?" he asked, and the tone of his voice had changed.

It was the tone that made her mouth go dry.

"Yeah," she said, and her voice was softer, sweeter, just something about the way he was looking at her made her want to curl up in his arms. Again.

They stared at each other for a bit before he blinked. She had the feeling he wanted to say something, but he shifted and looked down at his hands as though just remembering that he carried something.

"Oh yeah. I have this."

"That's your binder for work?"

"Yeah. You don't think I'm going to let you buy an inn and I'm not going to landscape it for you, do you?"

"I might not have money to pay for that. I... I want to do it eventually, of course."

"And you're not going to pay for it. After all, a man can hardly charge his wife when he does work for her, can he?"

"I'm sure there are husbands who can and do that very thing," she said with more than a little irony in her voice.

"This husband is not," he said, and there was no room for argument in his tone.

"Thank you," she said, in that voice she hardly recognized. She didn't even know she could talk like that. But these new feelings she felt for Mark brought it out in her.

"You want to go upstairs? We can sit on the floor, look at this, and I brought some food for us. I was going to warm up the casserole that Miss Lana brought us, but I made us subs instead."

"You make the best subs," she said, her stomach growling at the thought.

"I left them on the passenger seat."

"I'll grab them," she said, running around to the side and getting the subs that sat on the seat along with the water beside them.

He pulled his work laptop out from behind his seat, and they walked into the inn together, her smiling the entire way. There was just something about someone being so thoughtful that made her feel...cherished, almost.

Maybe that was the way a wife was supposed to feel. She wouldn't know; she'd never felt like this in her first marriage. Her first husband had been very much about himself, his hobbies, and making sure that he got what he deserved out of their relationship, and far less concerned about giving anything in return.

They admired the view while they ate, mostly in silence. A comfortable silence. The kind she always had with Mark.

Maybe he was thinking about plans and designs and all the possibilities for the inn. Probably she should be, too, but she wasn't.

She was thinking about how much she loved his strong jaw. The laugh wrinkles around his eyes and mouth. The fact that he knew exactly how she liked her sub and made it just that way for her - extra mayo and pickles, light on the meat and cheese and lots of onions.

More than the sub, though, she thought about how much she didn't want to be just friends. Didn't want her marriage with Mark to be only about sitting together and talking and easy silences with separate rooms.

Could she tell him?

"Pam?" he said, interrupting her thoughts as he brushed off his hands after finishing the last of his sub.

"Hmm?" she said, trying to bite down on her tongue. She didn't want to ruin what they had together.

"I think that even if your mother never gives you the inheritance, you'll have enough money from all the pledges to go ahead with your charter school. You'll probably never make a ton of money with it-"

"I don't care!"

"I didn't think you did."

"And it's us. We'll have enough money from all the pledges. This is not just me."

His grin was slow and sweet. "I'm good with that."

"I think when two people get married, they become one."

"That's what the Bible says."

"So, if I have an inn, we do."

"And if I have a landscaping business, we do."

"Well, you had that before we were married."

"It doesn't matter. Two become one."

She swallowed. Now was her chance to tell him how she really felt. But her mouth wouldn't work.

"You know, you could still hire a lawyer and get your inheritance. It would take them two seconds-"

"I can't. I don't even want to consider it. I don't want to take my mom to court. The Bible says we shouldn't take other Christians to court."

He sighed in a way that let her know that he wasn't entirely sure her mother was actually a Christian. She couldn't argue with that. She wasn't sure herself.

"She'll give me the money eventually." That she was sure of. Her mother was a lot of things, but a thief was not one of them.

"I admire your patience. I'm not sure I'd want to wait."

"I'd rather never get the money and still have a relationship with my mom. Even if it isn't the greatest. Even if she's not perfect and we'll never have the close re-lationship I dream about, I'd rather have what I can than ruin it fighting in court."

Mark looked down at his lap, like her words had made him think. Or like he disagreed and didn't want to argue. So much for the perfect time to tell him how she felt. She'd totally ruined the mood. If they'd even had a "mood."

"Pam?"

"Yeah?" She held her breath. Was he going to demand that since he was her husband, he could make her go after the money? Mark wouldn't. She was pretty sure he wouldn't, anyway.

"I love you." He grunted and looked away. "That was clunky and awkward." He lifted his head and looked her in the eye while his hand landed on her knee as she sat crossed legged on the floor. "I told you when we started this that I didn't want us to ever be anything more than friends because that would ruin everything, but I seem to have not listened to myself. I don't expect you to say or do anything, but I can't keep pretending I'm not spending most of the time we're together thinking about kissing you."

That made her blink. Then blink some more. He'd said he loved her. She thought he was talking about a friendship kind of love where he disagreed with what she was doing but admired her for it anyway.

Wow. She had been way off the mark. Her palms started to sweat.

Mark thought about kissing her.

"You could stop thinking about it and just do it," she whispered, although she wasn't sure where those words came from. Her heart and soul, maybe, since she wanted him to kiss her with her entire being.

He leaned closer. "Really?" he said, surprise and maybe a little relief coloring his tone.

"Really," she said, leaning toward him, making it easier, or maybe taking matters into her own hands. He's said she was patient, but that was only about money. When it came to Mark, she found she didn't want to wait. Or maybe she'd spent enough time waiting. "I hoped you were going to do it this morning before you got out of bed."

"I thought I scared you."

"Maybe you did. Just a little."

"I hope not."

"I didn't want you to know how I felt. Since you were so adamant that we had to be friends and nothing more."

"I changed my mind."

"I think I'm the one who's supposed to do that." She paused. "But I'm glad you did."

They were so close their lips almost brushed as they spoke and his breath flowed over her, warm and perfect. And when he moved just a bit closer, their mouths met and she closed her eyes, unable to contain her sigh.

Her fingertips buzzed and she put her hand around Mark's neck, pulling him closer, holding on as the world tilted and swayed and she pressed closer, wanting the heat of his body and to somehow be closer, even though her lungs had trouble working and her brain was still trying to process the fact that she was kissing her best friend.

He pulled away first, but she was pretty sure it was only because he was having the same trouble breathing that she was.

"I love you," she whispered.

He grinned. "I said it first."

"It isn't a competition," she said, with a small smile that most likely clearly showed that it actually was a competition. "I'll say it more."

"Okay," Mark grinned. He leaned forward and kissed her again and it was a long time until they disentangled themselves from each other and went home.

Chapter 22

"I don't want to go in." Pam met Mark on the sidewalk in front of the duplex. They'd had a really nice afternoon and evening at the inn, kissing, yes, but they also walked around outside and talked about the landscaping. They'd had a few phone calls and a couple more pledges from business owners in the area who wanted to put money toward the school.

Mark found himself unable to stop smiling. And unable to stop looking forward to that night when he'd be sharing his room with Pam...his wife.

"Why not?" he asked.

She pressed her lips together and he faced her on the walk. Pam's mother was a pill, but Pam didn't usually have trouble facing her.

"I'm not sure. I guess...all along we've been trying to convince them that we are really together, but somehow...this feels so new and precious..." She paused, as though she were a little embarrassed to call what they shared precious.

He took both of her hands in his and tugged gently, pulling her toward him until she pressed close and he was able to put his arms around her, holding her against his chest, loving the way they seemed made to fit together.

"It feels that way to me, too," he said, lying his cheek on the top of her head and wishing their house did not have other people in it. He wanted alone time with his wife. Maybe that's what she was saying, too.

"I guess I love the way it feels when we're like this and I don't want the world to intrude and ruin it. And my mother always intrudes."

He grunted a laugh, but tried not to snort. After all, Lynn was Pam's mother and Pam loved her. If he and Pam had become one through their marriage, he should love Lynn solely because Pam did.

"She loves you," he said, unable to think of anything else kind to say about her, but purposing in his heart that he would do his very best to not say anything negative about someone that Pam loved.

"I want her to love you, too."

"Maybe in her own way, she does." He wanted to add that he hoped she'd give in and give Pam her inheritance, but if he wasn't saying anything negative, that probably shouldn't leave his mouth.

"I love you," she whispered, leaning her head back to look into his eyes.

He took advantage of her position, to lean down and press his lips to hers.

He didn't mean for it to become a long kiss, but she sighed into his mouth and he deepened the kiss and totally forgot they were standing on the sidewalk in the dark in front of their duplex where his sister and her mother and his nieces and her daughters were all waiting for them to come home.

A light turned on and he'd just processed that when a voice said, "I told you it was real."

He pulled back, his breath shaky, his hands still clinging to his wife, and he wasn't sure who was helping who keep their balance as they turned, their arms around each other to face six pair of female eyes standing on their porch looking down the steps at them.

"You don't need to say I told you so." Lynn gave Ginger a narrowed-eye look.

"Well, I did." Ginger crossed her arms over her chest.

"So did I," Marilyn said.

"And me." Hilda pursed her lips.

"I knew it all along," Kay added.

"I couldn't have been the only one who was clueless," Paulette said, irritation in her voice, but there was a smile there, too.

"No. You weren't. I was as well." Lynn lifted her chin. "It looks like I need to transfer your inheritance to your account. I'll get on that in the morning." She started to turn. "Now, get in the house. It's uncouth to stand outside on the sidewalk

putting on that kind of display for anyone to see."

"It's dark out," Ginger said.

"It doesn't matter. The sidewalk is no place for such things." Lynn pulled the door open and held it, waiting for every-one to file in.

"I think Pam and I are just going to go in on my side." Mark normally would have asked her, but they'd been kissing and he'd been enjoying it and he kind of wanted to go someplace where he could keep kissing his wife without the censoring presence of her mother.

Lynn opened her mouth.

"Yes. We're newlyweds," Pam said be-fore her mother could say anything, grabbing his hand and pulling him up the stairs. She opened the door to his side of the duplex without saying anything to her mother, and held the door so he could go through.

"Good night, Mom," he couldn't help saying as he passed Lynn, then winked at Pam as he stepped into the house. She had a big, goofy, happy smile on her face.

"Good night, Mom," she echoed as she stepped in behind him and closed the door. It hadn't even clicked closed before he turned and swept her up in his arms, kissing her with everything in him, wanting her to know she was everything he'd ever wanted and he'd spend the rest of his life trying to show her how much he loved her.

He wasn't sure if he was successful in showing her all that, but she seemed to enjoy their evening just as much as he did, and he figured that was something, anyway. Maybe the rest of it would come in time. He could be patient.

Enjoy this preview of There I Find Wisdom, just for you!

Chapter 1

Lord, I don't know what I'm going to do.

Dakota Esenwein stayed on her knees beside the bed of her grandmother. It was one o'clock in the morning, or somewhere thereabouts. No sound permeated the house, except for her grandmother's breathing, and for all intents and purposes, she was alone.

Her children, at six and eight years of age, were too young to understand that this would be the last night their grandmother was with them on earth. Maybe they weren't too young to understand, but they were too young to keep an all-night vigil.

Dakota had tucked them into bed hours ago, knowing they probably wouldn't have a grandmother in the morning.

Or a place to stay.

They wouldn't be out that fast, but it was coming.

Dakota's sister, Kylie, was set to inherit the house.

Dakota had nothing. Not since her divorce, where her husband basically took everything she had.

Yellowstone Gold, her golden Palomino whom she called Goldie, was all Dakota had left in the world, other than a run-down store her grandmother would leave for her once she passed. In order for her to make ends meet, she was going to have to sell Goldie. She loved her horse, but she couldn't allow her children to starve.

She didn't regret her children, but she did regret her marriage.

But she had learned, over the years, that she couldn't live with regrets.

"Kota?"

Her gram's husky voice slid through Dakota's thoughts, and she squeezed the hand she held, lifting her head and peering through the darkness toward the head of the bed.

"Gram?"

Gram had been asleep the entire day before. She hadn't eaten or drunk anything in two days. Dakota had been putting chapstick on her lips to keep them from drying out, but her grandma had refused all ice chips or even a sip of water.

The hospice nurse had said it wouldn't be long.

"Don't forget about the gift shop."

How could she forget?

They knew the contents of the will. Her sister had been given the house. She had been given a worthless, run-down, out-of-business gift shop, with no inventory, in a nowhere town called Strawberry Sands.

It wasn't that she was so upset about it, or that she felt like it was unfair. She didn't expect her gram to give her anything, and she appreciated the fact that her gram felt like she had divided her assets equally between Kylie and Dakota.

The issue was, Dakota couldn't do anything with the gift shop. She wasn't a shopkeeper. She had no desire to live in Michigan. Even if it was a picturesque town beside the lake.

She loved her home in Iowa, such as it was. Since she'd lived with her gram since her divorce.

"Kota," her grandma prompted, unable to get her full name out.

"I won't. I promise, Gram," she said automatically. She wasn't going to forget about it, she just wasn't going to do anything with it. Except... Except she needed to do something.

She had to have a place to live. Kylie and she got along well, but Kylie was expecting Dakota to move out when she inherited the house. Kylie had just gotten married to a man who had three children, and they were planning on living right here.

They hadn't moved in because Dakota was here, and she had been the one taking care of Gram. Kylie had been decent enough to not kick Dakota out while their gram was dying.

Of course, she didn't exactly have that right, not until Gram breathed her last. Since Gram owned the house and would never make Dakota leave.

"Move there," her gram said weakly.

"Move where?" Dakota asked, blinking and coming back to the present. She wanted to savor every last interaction with her grandmother. Maybe she was wrong. Maybe her gram would last longer than what they thought. But the fact that she hadn't eaten, hadn't drunk, hadn't spoken in two days, and now...

Now she was going to talk? Dakota should listen.

"To the souvenir shop. Move there."

"Okay, Gram." She wanted to argue. How was she supposed to live in a shop?

"Live above it," Gram said weakly. "Where you stayed with me in the summer."

Dakota vaguely remembered the shop from visiting during the summer when she was a kid. She'd kind of forgotten that there was an apartment above the shop where her gram lived. She could hardly believe it, since she'd stayed there herself. But she hadn't realized that the apartment was part of the shop. She supposed in her head she had thought that her gram had rented the apartment. Or something.

She hadn't paid much attention to what was going on at the shop, because Strawberry Sands had a riding stable, and she had been as wild and free as she could be on the beach with the horses.

But that thought brought her pain too. Because it reminded her of Ryan Landry.

Ryan, whom she'd asked to marry her and who had turned her down. That was why she had ended up with Gregory, her ex.

But she wasn't going there either. She pushed the bad thoughts aside. She couldn't focus on the things that didn't work out. She had to focus on the things that she could control.

Which felt like very little. Except, she still had Goldie. For now.

She could put Goldie up on social media for sale, and she would sell within the hour. Dakota was confident of that. But Goldie had been the one constant that she'd had since her college days. Goldie had been with her as she became a championship contender, had been her best friend, had been the one that she told everything to, as her world came tumbling down, not twice but three times.

First, when her parents had been killed in a freak rodeo accident, and second when she felt like her only choice was to get married, and then again when her marriage imploded.

"I love you," her gram said weakly.

"Gram, I love you too. I wish you weren't leaving me." Boy, how she ever wished her gram wasn't leaving. It felt like everything in her life that she tried to hold onto had been ripped from her.

Everything except her children and Goldie.

"If I didn't leave, you couldn't move on to what's next. Don't be afraid. You know God has everything under control. Just follow His plan."

It was the most Gram had said to her in over a week, but she wanted to snort. It felt like God's plan for her whole life had been to kick her, then kick her harder. And anytime she tried to get up, He'd kick her again.

That felt like a really great sum of God's plan.

But somehow through all that, she never forgot He loved her. She never doubted it. Even though at times it felt like she should. Like the wise thing to do would be to just throw in the towel and admit that if there was a God, she didn't really want to know Him.

Except for the thought that all the bad things that she had gone through had made her stronger and better, had helped her become the person God wanted her to be, so that she could do what God wanted her to do, and she just couldn't let go of Him.

Maybe He really did have a plan for her.

She wanted to believe that. Sometimes, the things that a person really wanted to believe were the hardest things of all.

But she could hardly move forward with God's plan when she had no money, no place to live, and nothing to fall back on, with her gram leaving her.

Except for Goldie. She had Goldie.

The thought made her almost physically sick, but if she was going to move to Michigan, the only way that was going to happen was if she sold her horse.

As a grand champion barrel racing contender, Goldie was well known on the rodeo circuit, and even though she was past her prime and would not be winning any championships, she would be prized as a broodmare. Which is what

Dakota had planned for her, if she'd ever been able to have a place where Goldie could stay.

Currently, she was boarding Goldie and was two months behind on her payments to the stable owner.

The stable owner knew her gram was dying, and had given her grace, but Dakota couldn't promise to pay, because she had no idea how she was even going to feed her children, let alone board her horse.

She had to face the fact that as a responsible mother, it was more important that her children eat than that she keep her horse.

With that thought in her head, and with her gram's hand going limp, Dakota put her forehead back down on her gram's bed, still on her knees, and prayed again, "Lord, I don't want to let her go."

But a peace came to her, and while it wasn't an audible voice, she understood that what she had just thought—selling her horse and moving to Michigan—was the right thing to do.

Why does life have to be so hard, Lord? Are You really asking me to give up Goldie? She's the last thing I have, other than my children.

She needed to be grateful that God wasn't requiring her children.

I've given You everything. Everything except for them.

And Goldie.

She sighed. If she claimed to love God, if she claimed to be a follower of Christ, if she claimed to want God's glory and not her own, then giving up her horse shouldn't be such a struggle. It should be something she gladly did, if it furthered God's plan in her life. It shouldn't be something that was pried out of her cold, resisting fingers.

Gram's breathing changed, becoming harsher, harder, and Dakota lifted her head.

It was a shift that she immediately knew signaled the end.

She grabbed her phone and texted her sister.

Gram is leaving us.

Her sister probably wouldn't come, but she wanted to give her that option. She didn't want to keep her from being with her grandma at the end if she truly wanted to be. Although, they had known for the last several days that any minute could be her last.

And her last words had been to Dakota, telling her to move to Michigan. How could she tell her no? How could she deny her, even if it meant selling her beloved horse?

Her phone buzzed.

Thanks for letting me know. Tell me when she's gone, and I'll call the funeral director.

Dakota stared at her phone. At least Kylie was going to take care of that.

They'd already made plans; their gram had even helped. She didn't want a big funeral, didn't want a lot of fanfare, just wanted to be laid to rest as inexpensively as possible without being cremated. Being cremated was too much like going to hell, she said, and she didn't see it in the Bible as a viable thing; it was something that the heathens did. Whether it was or wasn't, they would pay a little extra to give her a traditional burial.

And Kylie would handle it. She would pay for it out of Gram's savings and no doubt pocket the rest.

That was fine with Dakota. She just wished her grandma hadn't needed to go. But God's timing was perfect, and

God was calling her home, and there was nothing Dakota could do to stop it.

She held her breath as Gram's breathing became unsteady, rough and loud.

Maybe being on her knees was the proper position, because it was like she could feel the angels coming to carry her grandmother home. Whether they were, whether they weren't, it felt like a sacred thing to be in the presence of someone who stepped from this world into the next.

She held tightly to Gram's hand, knowing that wouldn't keep her, and listened as Gram exhaled. Several dozen seconds later, she inhaled again, and this time, when she breathed out, everything was still.

Dakota let out the breath she had been holding. Just like that, her gram was gone.

And just like that, a new chapter of her life would begin.

Pick up your copy of There I Find Wisdom by Jessie Gussman today!

newsletter – I laughed so hard I sprayed it out all over the table!"

Claim your free
book from Jessie!